Imagine Their Courage

Honoring Bible Women

Study Guide

By

Scott Milner

About This Book

Title - Imagine Their Courage
Subtitle - Honoring Bible Women
Topic - Exploring the courage of Bible women.

Copyright © 2018 Scott Milner
All rights reserved.

Front Cover - Christina, always a princess.

Acknowledgements

Thanks to God for allowing me to share.
Thanks to my wife Sharon who encouraged me every day to proceed and publish.
Thanks to the women in the Bible who courageously seized the day and teach us how.
Thanks to the women of today who live out the values of the Bible and show us how.
A special thanks to my editors and, Sharon, Boyd, Gena, Lori, Tanya, and Karla.

All Bible references are taken from the NIV unless otherwise noted.

Books by this author:

<u>Paperback</u>

Imagine Their Courage – Study Guide

<u>Kindle E-books</u>

Eve wants us to Know, what she saw

Imagine Their Courage

Introduction

This book explores the events, risks, and the breath taking victories of courageous women in the Bible. While we read through their stories we are treated to extraordinary moments where we gradually, or suddenly, realize how astonishing they were. They endured hardships and celebrated triumphs equal to, or stronger than, those of the men in their time, and they should be applauded. They were very brave and determined, stood up for loved ones, and valiantly opposed colossal dangers. Even with little authority, and not much respect, many of them caused or changed history with their words and actions. Today, thousands of years later, we still learn from them. They are the mothers, sisters, advisors, best friends, and guardians of all who follow. We are privileged to honor each and recognize their contributions.

When you and I examine their lives we can step into their time and employ all five of our senses. With flexible imaginations we can visualize what the environment was like. What do we hear or see? What is the temperature, and what do we smell? Is there an atmosphere of chaos or a calm serenity? Can we feel the positive emotions erupting there; such as awe, joy, love, and gratitude, or do we shudder under the weight of negative sensations like fear, sleeplessness, and panic?

Let's embark on a journey to examine the real, and the probable, activities in the lives of exceptionally daring women in the Bible. Their accounts take us to a day, year, or decade when they faced enormous struggles: poverty, capture, loss of family, slavery, famine, transfer, or worse. Security could fluctuate daily. There were few laws and no police to protect citizens, especially women. A woman could wake each day uncertain of whom she would belong to that night. Others were thrust into roles of prominence which brought their own type of responsibility and/or conflict. They prayed with soul wrenching sincerity, talked with angels, sat as queens, and witnessed miracles. These women performed and survived with such bold significance that God wanted us to know them, and He included their stories in the Bible. The primary source of this exploration is referenced Bible scripture. The secondary source is our imaginations, yours and mine, emerging from our intuitions and experiences.

Many of the stories we read in the Bible are brimming with detail, others are so concise we find ourselves yearning for more information about what else happened. The brief accounts may describe highlights of an important event but share little else, and that leaves us wondering. An excellent example of this is found in the book of Judges, chapter four. A woman named Jael kills Sisera, the commander of an army opposed to Israel, while he lies sleeping in her tent. It is a very dramatic event; serious consequences will result from her success, or her failure. Yet, her full story and her efforts only fill seven verses of the Bible. We know nothing more about her beyond the moment she changes history by driving a tent peg through the head of Sisera with a hammer. Notice what happens if we pause at the end of the report and think it through.

Pretty quickly we begin to wonder about Jael and a lot of questions surface. They might sound like this: How did she get the idea and courage to kill Sisera? How did she act her part so well that her true intentions remained totally hidden from him? Was she naturally aggressive enough to kill or did this traumatic event change her? As she approached him with her weapon, did she panic or tremble, have second thoughts, or doubt her chances?

Then, what do we do with these questions? We guess and ponder; what did that situation look and feel like? Imagine standing there, listening for every sound, watching Sisera quietly breathing, slowly advancing, concealing the weapon until the very moment of attack, and then striking with full adrenaline powered vengeance. In that story and dozens of others, there awaits enormous opportunities for us to apply conjecture and enjoy the probable actions and adventure we presume.

There are positive benefits in the practice of using presumption to fill in the blank spots. We may embrace a person and their events and make them more real to us, and more memorable. While I find that this is a valuable endeavor, we must always employ caution. Where the Bible passes over periods of time in the life of someone, we may contemplate about what they were doing and try to piece it together, but thoughtfully and with great respect. We must not dream up and then hold as certain truth, activities or conversations that in any way alter a single word in the Bible. We do not have the wisdom or authority to make any changes to written scripture. Also, we must not exaggerate or reduce the quality of the people, or the strength of the message, in the story. If we imagine a day or moment in the life of a Bible character, our speculations must be tested to see if, during or after their inclusion, the message of the Bible remains exactly the same as before.

The Bible is ours to insert ourselves into. Our spirit prompts us to examine the situations, learn the lessons, memorize the promises, and embrace its wisdom. The Bible is available to us to hold up high as our guide and love from God, and with it we explore and dream.

The purpose of this book is not to be a detailed, precise research into theology. I do not have the credentials for that. Instead, the purpose of this book is to explore and emphasize the accomplishments of several women in the Bible so we can understand them better and say, "Wow, they were really special." I do have the credentials for that, and so do all of you. All you need is some dedicated time reading the Bible and a brave unbridled imagination.

Now, let me explain the arrangement of this book. There are sixteen chapters. With the exception of two, each chapter addresses one distinctive woman. Chapter seven concerns two sisters, and chapter sixteen focuses on all women past and present, who seek to follow God and give their best to themselves, their family, and their community. Each chapter is presented with an introduction and five labeled sections. Descriptions of each section with a short example are found below.

Introduction – I start each chapter with a prologue where we briefly meet a woman and step into her world. At the start of each introduction you see a date that represents an approximation to when the events occurred.

Section one. Bible account – This is a verse by verse examination of a woman's story from the Bible. These are written in summarized paraphrases, and therefore, you should read your preferred version of the Bible to study the actual text.

Since this is a study guide, immediately following the Bible account there are two pages of questions in each chapter.

Section two. Lessons – This is where we look for helpful and inspirational lessons we can identify, study, and apply.

Section three. Imagine That – I propose possibilities about conditions or events involving the woman, and though not written down, they were likely in the quiet gaps of the Bible account. Also in this section, we recognize, highlight, and honor each woman's strengths and contributions.

Section four. A Short Narrative – This is a "fictional" story of an episode in the life of a woman. This is mostly a fantasy, but very probable, and is based on Bible scripture, plus conjecture and intuition. The intention is to consider a possible situation in their lives and join them there. This can be enlightening and just fun.

Section five. Conclusion – A review to emphasize and retain the major contributions and triumphs.

Let me take you through a brief example of these five sections using the story of the day when Moses was hidden in a basket to save his life.

Moses' Mother

Introduction – 1525 BC

Moses' mother was a slave in Egypt. The Pharaoh of Egypt gave an order that all Hebrew baby boys must be thrown into the Nile. Instead, when Moses was a baby his mother placed him in a basket and hid him along the shore of the Nile River. The Pharaoh's daughter found the basket and paid his actual mother to nurse and care for him.

Bible account

The story of baby Moses is found in Exodus chapter two.

Realizing she could no longer hide her baby, Moses' mother placed him in a basket and hid him among the reeds on the shore of the Nile. (2:3)
When Pharaoh's daughter went to the Nile to bathe, she found Moses. (2:5-6)
Moses' sister offered to find a Hebrew woman to nurse the baby. (2:7)
Pharaoh's daughter paid Moses' mother to nurse her own baby. (2:8-9)

Study Question

1. Can we guess that Moses' mother had a vision from God, because it is rather risky to put your child in a basket and cast him adrift on a river with nothing more than hope that he will be okay?

_____
_____

Lesson

God knows very well when we make sacrifices and risk ourselves to protect others, and often turns events back to our benefit.

Imagine That

Moses' mother risked her own life to protect the life of Moses. She knew if she were caught concealing the baby, she would probably be executed. The hovering uncertainty, and the surprise result, challenged and comforted her heart with great fervor.

God honored her sacrifice and set up the paradox. He arranges for Pharaoh's daughter to pay Moses' mother to nurse her own baby.

A Short Narrative

For weeks, at home, Moses' mother has been careful, quickly quieting Moses when he makes sounds. Now she is afraid of detection and plans to hide him safely. In the early morning dark hours she slowly tiptoes among the shadows working her way to the thick reeds on the shore of the Nile. Once there, crouching down, she is crying, apologizing, cuddling, praying, praising, shaking, watchful, and heartbroken. God is with her; she will get her son back to treasure for a season. God intervenes allowing her precious time as a mother.

Conclusion

Moses' mother was valiant. To circumvent the Pharaoh's order, she hides her baby boy. She risked her life to conceal him at the Nile. She is terrified for herself and Moses; she is also very brave. Imagine her courage. She is successful and Moses survives, grows up, and goes on to lead Israel out of slavery.

As you read this book and the Bible account of each woman, insert yourself into each story. Consider the weight of the situation each lady is facing. Stand beside her and listen, regard the urgency and the hazards, reason through the choices available, and then watch her face and listen to her words. Whether she encounters agony or ecstasy, imagine her strength, imagine her courage, and celebrate her triumph.

Table of Contents

Heroine	Page
Abigail	8
Bathsheba	15
Elizabeth	22
Esther	29
Eve	37
Hannah	47
Lot's Daughters	53
Mary	60
Naomi	68
Rahab	75
Ruth	85
Samson's mother	93
Sarah	100
Vashti	107
Veronica	113
You	120

Closure

Summary	126
List of Lessons	127

Abigail

Introduction – 1020 BC

Abigail is married to a man named Nabal, a wealthy man who owns large flocks, but her circumstances are about to change. Pretty soon she will instead be married to the man who as a shepherd killed lions with his bare hands, and who will one day be the king of Israel.

The Bible tells us Abigail is wise, wealthy, and beautiful. She is married to Nabal who will soon die because of his disrespect, and lack of gratitude, regarding David, the man who killed Goliath with a stone. David is on course to kill Nabal, but when Abigail intercedes, David backs off. Then God takes charge and Nabal dies.

We meet Abigail while David is preparing four hundred of his six hundred soldiers to attack and kill Abigail's husband and all the men in his family. We follow her actions as she hurriedly prepares to deliver a peace offering on her husband's, and David's, behalf. She must act quickly because David is determined to take vengeance before daybreak.

Abigail is influential and brave and takes command of a dangerous situation, proceeding to defuse the wrath of four hundred aggressive soldiers. She understands God's intentions for David and appeals to David's sense of justice. She is a prudent woman; she prevents senseless slaughter, honors the future King of Israel, and makes everyone see the situation through the eyes of God. Abigail is an astonishing woman.

Bible account of Abigail in 1st Samuel chapter twenty five.

Abigail is the wife of Nabal. Theses verses say Nabal is wealthy and has flocks and property in Carmel. They also say Nabal is surly and mean, but Abigail is intelligent and beautiful. (25:2-3)

David is on the run, leading six hundred men and seeking provisions for them. He hears that Nabal is in Carmel shearing sheep and he knows Nabal is wealthy and can afford to help them. Additionally, David and his men recently provided protection for Nabal's shepherds and flocks, so some expression of gratitude in the form of food is anticipated and proper. (25:4-9)

Nabal listens to the request of David's messengers, but refuses to help them and then insults the messengers and questions their honesty. (25:10-11)

David did not appreciate Nabal's reply and prepares to execute Nabal and every male belonging to him. (25:12-13, 21-22)

One of Nabal's servants informs Abigail about the visit from David's men, their request, and Nabal's response. The servant also defends David's request as reasonable and asks her to consider the proper approach to take. (25:14-17)

Abigail understands the validity of David's request, the urgency motivating her servant's report, and the importance of her acting quickly. (25:18-19)

Coincidence here must be divine intervention. Abigail is riding into the mountain ravine where David and his men are headed in her direction. Just before she arrives, David makes his pledge to the Lord, "May God deal with me severely if I leave any male alive in the house of Nabal." (25:20-22)

Abigail approaches David with gifts, humility, and explanations. She appeals to his sense of justice and honor. (25:23-27)

Abigail declares God will give David a lasting throne. She appeals to David to behave in ways that don't damage the dignity of the realm. Then she offers a blessing that all of David's enemies would be as insignificant as Nabal. (25:28-31)

David realizes she is right and thanks Abigail for good judgment and praises God for sending her, which kept David from bloodshed. David accepts her gifts and sends her home in peace. (25:32-35)

Abigail waits until he is sober, to tell Nabal all that has happened. When she finally tells him, his heart fails him and in ten days he dies. (25:36-38)

David sends word asking Abigail to be his wife and she consents. (25:39-42)

Study Questions

1. When Abigail realized her family was at risk of harm she took steps to solve the issue. Describe a situation where you have witnessed or acted with similar strength and judgment. How much self confidence would a woman need to see it through?

   _____
   _____
   _____

2. How do you see Abigail applying the principles of Romans 12:18? Describe situations where you have done the same.

   _____
   _____
   _____

3. Why didn't Abigail discuss with her husband that she wanted to take food to David and his men?

   _____
   _____
   _____

4. David and his 600 soldiers are on the run, hiding wherever they can, and hunted constantly by King Saul's soldiers. Why do you suppose King Saul's soldiers couldn't find David and his men, but Abigail could? Imagine the courage Abigail needed to take food to the camp of an angry outlaw and have only servants to act as her escorts.

   _____
   _____
   _____

5. How do we know Abigail respected but did not follow the God of the Israelites?

   _____
   _____
   _____

6. Explain the main points in Abigail's appeal, 1 Sa 25:28-31, to persuade David not to kill her husband.

7. Where can we find evidence of Abigail's humility, and what were her actions?

8. When Abigail told her husband, Nabal, about giving David food and how it saved Nabal's life, he fell into something like a coma for ten days. Describe the stress and apprehension you imagine Abigail endured every one of those days. How might she have reacted after Nabal died and before David proposed?

9. David sent word to Abigail to become his wife. He was offering a life on the run, hiding with an outlaw and 600 men, fearful of capture and battles every day. Why do you think she said yes?

10. Abigail was kidnapped by the Amalekites and the rescued by David (1 Sa 30:1-5 & 18). Put yourself in Abigail's shoes the first couple of weeks after she was rescued. How do you think she felt about this life on the run with an outlaw and, oh by the way, he has another wife?

Lessons

1. Just like Abigail, we are to be peacemakers. David's son Solomon writes, "A gentle answer turns away wrath" (Pr 15:1). Paul wrote, "If it is possible, as far as it depends on you, be at peace with everyone" (Ro 12:18). Abigail is applying these wise principles to honor the future king, demonstrate humility, and make the best attempt at last minute negotiations.
2. If a conflict is possible, it is best to approach it directly and swiftly rather than ignore it and hope it goes away. Matthew wrote, "Settle matters quickly with your adversary before it gets worse" (Mt 5:25).
3. Be ready at all times to express gratitude and help people. Here we can find a parallel between Jesus and David. David protects Nabal's resources, and Jesus protects ours. David asked Nabal to give some of his resources, Jesus asks us to give some or ours, with our tithing and time. They are both kings; Abigail knew you don't turn down the king who protects you. Maybe Jesus won't send ten men to stand before you and ask for food, but He might send one or two. "Do not forget to show hospitality to strangers, for by so doing some people have shown hospitality to angels without knowing it" (He 13:2).

Imagine That

Just Imagine Abigail's –

Confidence – She behaves as if she has authority to use the family's vast supplies at her discretion. When the servant informs her about Nabal offending David's men, she doesn't ask permission to take supplies or consult her husband in any way. She moves with influence, without delay or hesitation, as if she is the primary person in charge and an outcome of success or disaster, depends solely on her.

Diplomacy – She crafts a presentation to David calculated to honor him, benefit his men, and avert the execution of all the men in her family. She appeals to David's sense of justice, mercy, and conscience. She is a master negotiator and her argument leaves no room for disagreement. David wisely agrees with her after she reasons with him. Notice the points she makes. 1. Do not be offended by Nabal, he is a fool and not worth your effort. He isn't worth tarnishing your sword. 2. Since God has kept you from bloodshed, may you be so blessed that all your enemies are as insignificant as Nabal. 3. Since you will certainly be king it is important that you have a clear conscience free of any wrongdoing. Think about the national pride; our king is always brave, merciful, and just.

Wisdom – When she returns home after averting a near catastrophe, she realizes that this is not the time to rationalize with Nabal. He is confrontational when he is sober, but now he is even worse because he is drunk and impaired. He is celebrating and will not welcome any disagreeable news. This is not the time to tell him that a fair portion of his resources were donated to a hunted renegade. She carefully chooses to tell him her story after a night of rest so he might be more reasonable.

Determination – She responds swiftly to two important situations. First, when she takes food to David, and second, when she goes to become his wife. She selects and packs a significant offering to deliver. She doesn't send the offering, she takes it in person. She quickly gets off the donkey when she meets David (verse 23), and also, quickly gets on the donkey (verse 42) when it is time to go join David and become his wife.

Humility – She is wealthy, wise, and beautiful and has five female attendants, but when she meets David, she falls at his feet. She puts every other concern on hold, and immediately goes in person and subjects herself to David. Then, later when his servants come to suggest her marriage to David, she says she is willing to wash the feet of the servants. (1 Sa 25:41)

A Short Narrative

Imagine Abigail's courage.

Set your imagination to roughly 1020 BC and the early days of David, the future king of Israel. In the market squares rumors are whispered, "Samuel has anointed David to be king." However, David refuses to take the throne away from Saul, the reigning king of Israel. David will wait for God to remove him, but while he waits, King Saul attempts repeatedly to kill him. David now has over six hundred devoted men who follow his lead, and they move about together evading the king's soldiers. Evasion and concealment are challenging for six hundred men, and food supplies are crucial. David sends ten men to Nabal, a man with spare food, who certainly is indebted to David. Nabal refuses and insults David's men and the encounter is reported to Nabal's wife, Abigail.

Let's listen in as she rapidly reflects on what just happened. In swift succession some appalling realizations skip to and fro and sting her mind. "What? Did Nabal not know who those men were? David sent ten men here to ask for help, but we sent them away empty handed AND we insulted them!! They came representing the man who raced toward and killed the giant Goliath with a single stone; the David who protected our shepherds and flocks with his own soldiers, the man who the prophet Samuel anointed as the king of Israel; the man who killed lions with his bare hands. That David, sent men to us to ask for help and we gruffly told them to go away. Clearly Nabal has sentenced us all to a speedy death."

Abigail unmistakably understands their sudden dire situation and initiates a plan to prevent an impending disaster. She is about to look fear right in the eye and she won't even blink. This is when we witness inconceivable strength and courage. Abigail rides to face the danger with servants, not body guards or soldiers, but servants, to escort her. She is about to confront the future king of Israel who is accompanied by four hundred armed, hungry, angry, alert and on edge, battle proven men. None of them know she is coming to meet them and when she comes into view their adrenaline peaks out for defense of their king. They advance quickly to protect David and outflank the uncertain visitor. Is this a trap? Is this beautiful woman a decoy or distraction? Four hundred men scattered on uneven terrain posturing aggressively can be very intimidating. Their disposition as she arrives is composed of hostility prepared to rapidly kill and conquer. On her journey, has Abigail been rehearsing her apology and petition? She relies, not only for success in diplomacy, but for her very life, on the just mercy of a man who she knows is very, very, irritated. She knows she could be captured or killed in the time span of a breath. She does not shrink back or flee. She is not at a loss for words. As swiftly as possible she must soothe a desperate renegade, a rational man, a majestic king. Imagine her terror; imagine her courage.

David listens patiently as a man of integrity, as a man with the qualities of a king would. God blesses her effort and David accepts her counsel and gifts. As Abigail concludes her appeal to David she utters, possibly without knowing it, a prophecy of her own future. She says, "When the Lord has brought you success, remember your servant." King David, her future husband, certainly will remember her.

But before she sits comfortably in a palace as a wife of the king, some rough days lie ahead for her.

She has pacified the man who held her life in his hands and now must explain it to her husband. Nabal is celebrating the year's new wealth and is too far into his wine to listen to her. She hears his loud boasts and rejoicing; she will wait until he rests. The next day she describes the accounts she put together and Nabal realizes he lives only because of her actions; his heart fails him. For ten days he is alive, but non-responsive. Perhaps Nabal is not a pleasant man, but he is her husband. Abigail paces, talks to him, calls for doctors, holds his hand, and prays. God listens, but He has another plan. Nabal dies.

While Abigail is adjusting to the thoughts of grief, mourning, and widowhood, David sends messengers to ask her to be his wife. Abigail wastes no time accepting the offer and goes to David. This is a major shift in conditions for Abigail. She lived a pretty nice life of comfort with Nabal. Even though he was gruff, she had wealth and some stability. Now she will marry and hide with an outlaw. Frequently their shelter, food sources, security, and residence will fluctuate abruptly. Never sure when they would have to run, hide, or fight, Abigail's faith and patience are pulled tight. Any reflections on a nice hot bath, served meals, soft comforts, or privacy are parked for the future. And if these inconveniences did not test her fortitude enough, she gets kidnapped. (1 Sa 30)

Conclusion

How well can a person ride a donkey while her nerves are shaking like a nine on an earthquake scale? When Abigail got off the donkey to meet David she boldly took command of the circumstances. The weight of life or death for her husband and family rested on her actions and words. Her preparation, heart, wisdom, petitions, humble posture, and negotiations disarmed a king and four hundred warriors. Not a drop of blood was shed. We need a million more just like her today.

Abigail put two future Bible verses into action; when she approached David with supplies and later when she told her husband what had taken place. Romans 12:18 says, "If it is possible, as far as it depends on you, live at peace with everyone." Proverbs 15:1 says, "A gentle answer turns away wrath." Those are two outstanding guides to park in our memory and practice as often as possible. Abigail demonstrated what they look like and how they work and we will live much more calm lives if we imitate her. When stress and anxiety soar, calm down and choose gentle words.

Bathsheba

Introduction – 1000 BC

Perhaps Bathsheba needs no introduction, thanks to King David. Her story, David's big fall from honor, is very well known and thoroughly discussed among Bible readers everywhere. Unfortunately, that incident and the deception designed to cover the disgrace, are just about all that is remembered about Bathsheba. At the mention of her name, well entrenched opinions surface as sour groans. However, I bring attention to her to highlight her bravery and I give her a place of honor for facing and enduring some tough situations. Maybe she contributed to David's temptation, but no author in the Bible places any type of blame on Bathsheba. Grab a Concordance and you will see it is so. Her own son, King Solomon, honors her by bowing when she walks in and he sets up a throne for her. She was respected and loved.

Instead, consider for a moment why we should emphasize and admire her strength. She is taken, without being asked, twice by a king. In her life, she must face the loss of two husbands and her first son, all whose deaths submerge her in grief. Yet she carries on fulfilling roles as wife of a king, and then mother of a king. She is in the public eye, well-liked, pitied, envied, or ignored. Her first son with King David dies, and if their second son doesn't become king, he too may die. Bathsheba is resilient and is known in the roles of wife, mother, and grandmother of three consecutive kings.

Bible account of Bathsheba in 2nd Samuel

King David went for a walk in the evening and from the roof of the palace he saw a woman bathing on her roof. (11:2)

David learns she is Bathsheba, married to Uriah. He sends for her and sleeps with her.(11:3-4)

Bathsheba returns home and sends word to David, she is pregnant. (11:5)

David really hits his dark side here. He sends for Uriah, husband of Bathsheba, to come home from the battle fields and spend time with his wife. David hopes Uriah will sleep with Bathsheba and assume the baby is his. On his own initiative, Uriah does not go to his wife, not while the battle rages. (11:6-11)

David then softens Uriah with food and wine, hoping he would go home to his wife. But Uriah will not. (11:12-13)

David then changes tactics and arranges for Uriah to be placed in the most dangerous area of a battle. The battle ends the life of Uriah. (11:14-21)

David and Bathsheba learn of Uriah's death. Bathsheba mourns and then becomes David's wife. David's actions anger God. (11:22-27)

Nathan the prophet visits David with a parable, "A very greedy man acted in a very evil way." David replies the man must die. Nathan says, "You are the man." (12:1-12)

Nathan tells David the child born to Bathsheba will die. David pleads with God and fasts. Regardless, the child dies. (12:13-23)

David goes to Bathsheba and comforts her. She becomes pregnant again and gives birth to a boy they name Solomon. (12:24-25)

Bible account of Bathsheba in 1st Kings

David's fourth son, Adonijah, sets himself up as king, trying to supersede the elderly David and beat Solomon to the throne. (1:5-10)

Nathan the prophet tells Bathsheba about Adonijah and warns her to guard herself and Solomon from him. Then Nathan asks her to go to the King to ensure her son Solomon receives the throne as king by David's own proclamation. (1:11-14)

Bathsheba visits King David and he listens to her report. She tells him about the celebration Adonijah put on to announce his acceptance of the throne. (1:15-21)

Nathan the prophet arrives to tell King David the same report and asks for an explanation. (1:22-27)

Bathsheba pleases the king and he immediately energizes the process to put Solomon on the throne. Bathsheba thanks and praises the king. (1:28-31)

Study Questions

1. Did Bathsheba contribute to David's temptation? Consider 2 Sa 11:2 and 2 Sa 12:7-8

   No

2. Regarding Bathsheba, why did the author tell us in 2 Sa 11:4, "Now she was purifying herself from her monthly uncleanness?"

   Bathsheba — Wasn't Pregnant

3. According to Lev 20:10, both David and Bathsheba were to be put to death. How do you believe Bathsheba dealt with this law?

   Stoned — Can King be Stoned!

4. Bathsheba sent word to David, "I am pregnant", but then asked for nothing from him (2 Sa 11:5). Explain if you think she handled the situation in the best way?

5. While Bathsheba waited for a response from the king, what fears or hopes may have repeated in her thoughts regarding her husband and the king?

6. The king called Bathsheba's husband Uriah home from battle and ordered him to go home to her, but Uriah refused to go. How did the marriage between Bathsheba and Uriah end? How did the prophet Nathan respond?

   _____

   _____

   _____

7. Nowhere in the Bible is Bathsheba chastised for her role with David. How does that contribute to our perspective of her?

   _____

   _____

   _____

8. Bathsheba lost her husband and her first child within one year. She grieved and David comforted her, 2 Sa 12:24. What would you tell her or any woman, experiencing loss, regarding her prayers to God?

   _____

   _____

   _____

9. Bathsheba learned that her son Solomon was suddenly at risk of harm, 1 Kings 1:11-13. The news generated a burst of courage and motivated her to take protective action. Describe a time when fear for your loved ones provided you with courage that both surprised you and enabled your successful resolution.

   _____

   _____

   _____

10. The king knew two bad issues concerning Bathsheba. First, he caused the death of her husband; second, he knew about the prophecy from Nathan which foretold that the king's wives would be handed over to a relative, (2 Sa 12:11). How do think Bathsheba would respond to those two surprise and shocking reports?

    _____

    _____

    _____

Lessons

1. There is a parallel between Bathsheba and Mary, and between God and David; their only sons die and sin is taken away (2 Sa 12:13 – 14, 1 Co 15:3). God took David's son and God gave us His own son, and both times sin was removed.
2. Bathsheba did not judge David for the seduction, the pregnancy or the child's death. She probably expected God to take care of that and the same approach is to be observed by all of us. "Do not judge and you shall not be judged." (Lu 6:37)
3. Nothing is hidden from God. All of David's efforts advanced the error from bad to worse. He could have been the original source of the well known Sir Walter Scott quote, "What a tangled web of lies we weave, when we first choose to deceive." Since God knows what we are thinking (Ps 19:14) and planning, abandon any notion of concealing our iniquities. The deeper we bury our mistakes the harder it is to fix them. Do not run or hide, bring them all to God.

Imagine That

1. Bathsheba is courageous. She is summoned, seduced, impregnated, and dismissed by the king. That weighs heavy on her heart, mind, and conscience. She learns she is pregnant, knows she cannot place any demand on the father, and has no idea of what or how to tell Uriah. Then, her husband is killed in battle and the son she just gave birth to falls gravely ill and is expected to die. She faces the torment of the illness and then she must, in less than a year's time, mourn the loss of her husband and her only son. She survives, maybe with a lot of sleepless nights, but certainly with her spirit intact. Imagine her courage.
2. My Bible (NIV) has a footnote emphasizing 2 Sa 11:4. "She had just completed her cleansing." It is additional proof that David was the father. Why else would that be in the Bible?
3. Bathsheba probably learned about the circumstances of her husband Uriah's death before David died. It was available and important enough to show up in the Bible. Even so, for the rest of David's life, she remained in support of him.

A Short Narrative

Search through my memoirs and you will notice they mostly report, in detail, my two primary occupations. First, I enjoy raising Solomon and teaching him about nature, our history, nobility, and family. Second, I moderately participate in the administration of the appearance and activities of the Palace. My time with David is very limited for several reasons. He has other wives, several children, and well, he spends a lot of time running a nation of over a million loyal subjects. He is engaged with evictions of foreign gods and idols, training of new soldiers, executions, feasts with nobles and visiting dignitaries, and ruling in complicated cases of personal conflict. Some evenings I am David's primary concentration. Sometimes I don't cross his path for a week or a month; that is when I focus on Solomon and the Palace.

Decisions and plans regarding the palace are simple enough. We, the wives of the King, promote our own hopes for palace décor; sometimes we easily agree, but sometimes we squabble. Haggith is not so easy to compromise with. Abigail is the best. She supports, encourages, and nudges the rest of us with immense wisdom. Together we consider the amounts and varieties of foods for routine meals as well as for banquets. We also determine the appearance, protocol, and duties of the servants, the evening entertainment, components of music, rehearsals of heralds, and how best to honor our guests. When we cooperate, we choose adornments of the palace, you know, draperies, chairs, statues, and wall coverings or paintings. These interactions and options have kept me busy, and often quite satisfied.

Decisions regarding Solomon are almost entirely mine. I am pretty sure that is because David still harbors guilt about our first child. At first I chose Solomon's clothes, food, training, and activities. Then he matured to take over those selections and I enjoy the results. He and I shared numerous walks discussing nature and people for hours. He is very inquisitive. He could imagine a hundred questions I could answer and another hundred I couldn't. So, we researched and inquired together. It is great mother and son bonding time and a love of life sharing.

Now he is a young man and I am extremely proud of him. But today, just now something startling and new comes to me. Over the last many years I was seldom approached to give advice or counsel in major concerns of the kingdom. Also, rarely did it come into my best interest or preference to intrude in the weighty management of the throne. Now something profound and terrifying rests in my hands. I must decide and act quickly, immediately, and respectfully, but I am trembling.

Nathan, the prophet, comes to me with sudden and frightening news. Adonijah, the son of Haggith, put himself on the throne as king, to supersede his father, King David. Though David is older and slower now, the throne is still his, he is still the king, still in charge, and this takeover is not according to promises he made to Solomon and myself. David is unaware of Adonijah's overthrow and the momentum of his plans. Already heralds have announced the new king, and a banquet to honor him is in full vigor. Nathan appeals to me to intercede, so I really need some internal strength now.

I should not be surprised that Adonijah shoves himself in. For months now I have tolerated the same behavior from his mother, Haggith. She is always trying to possess the palace and take full control. If you watch her in action, bossing the servants, stomping about and raising her voice, and grabbing the post of honor at all banquets, you can so guess where her son gets his arrogance.

Nathan makes it clear that I must go to the king and respectfully negotiate for the right of Solomon to succeed David as king. Now let me just say right here for all future Bible readers, you all already know my endeavor will succeed. But, here in this minute, I don't know it yet and I am terrified of getting it wrong. This comes at me fast and I have very little practice in persuading kings. Failure will result in almost certain death by the call of Adonijah. Competition for the throne won't permit potential rivals. Close relatives who pose a threat are quickly eliminated. While I present my petition, Nathan arrives and I am ushered out while the king hears the report from his prophet. Now my terror soars. I must go out and wait, and my mind races through numerous possible outcomes. I breathe deep, pace, pray, shudder, pace more, and extract every ounce of courage I can. Every minute waiting multiplies my anxiety and deflates my confidence. Pace with me, hear my pulse pound, and imagine if you can, for me to stand up to this, imagine my courage. It surprises me too.

At last, King David calls me in and announces "Start the process to put Solomon on the throne now, today, immediately" (1 Ki 1:29 – 35). My grin is so intense it cramps my cheeks. I nearly faint, I nearly scream, tears of joy blur my vision, drench my cheeks, and drip from my chin, I pant like the race horse, my steps leap like the gazelle, and I hug everyone in sight. God chose Solomon to be king and made it so. Amen! Amen! Amen!

Conclusion

Bathsheba knew the disgrace of seeming to cheat her husband, and angering God. She felt the grief of outliving two husbands and one son. Conversely, she also experienced the thrill of fulfilling two exhilarating roles; first, as the wife of a king, and second, as the mother of a king. We can only imagine how challenging it was for her to stand strong to protect the lives of Solomon and herself. Little did she know she was directly in the family line that led to the savior of the world; our Lord Jesus Christ.

There are at least two solid reasons to argue that Bathsheba spent the last years of her life in peace. First, King David wrote an entire Psalm (Ps 51) recording his plea with God for forgiveness regarding his actions with Bathsheba and Uriah. The wording in Psalm 51 reveals David's confidence in God's forgiveness, which extends to Bathsheba as well when she prays. Second, Bathsheba's own son, King Solomon, installed a throne next to his, for his mother. From then on, she was beheld with honor, viewed with respect, and adorned with majesty.

Bathsheba goes on to give birth to three more sons by David (1 Ch 3:5). We may hope and expect one, two, or all three to bring great joy to her as she watches them grow, learn from her, and mature into strong and capable men.

Elizabeth

Introduction – 40 BC – 50 AD

Elizabeth is the wife of Zechariah and today he, chosen by lot, has the temple duties. She is curious and wondering; her husband is extraordinarily late returning from the temple. Finally he appears, but seems distant from her dozen questions and he is speechless. Her husband has good news and he just can't get it written down fast enough. At last, they will be parents, and their son will be someone very special.

Elizabeth reminds herself, "My son will be the number one herald of all time." He will announce the arrival of a king like no other. She is the mother of John the Baptist and suddenly one day, he will be filled with the Holy Spirit while still in her womb. Elizabeth will feel John kick her when she hears her relative Mary, the mother of Jesus, speak to her. Her son will intimately know the presence of God every moment, every day. He will introduce the world to God. We meet Elizabeth while she bravely endures the shame of barrenness. Then, we sit with her while she stills her breathing, to feel her child stretch inside. It is remarkable and she sighs, reigning in the pace of her heart and imagining the future of her son who will be "a voice of one calling in the wilderness." (Mark 1:3) Imagine Her Courage. Imagine Her Joy.

Bible account of Elizabeth in the book of Luke

Zechariah is a priest, his wife Elizabeth is not able to conceive, and they are both now very old. (1:5-7)

Zechariah is chosen by lot to enter the temple to burn the incense while worshippers pray outside. (1:8-10)

While burning incense in the temple, Zechariah is visited by an angel who tells him that he and his wife will soon have a son. (1:11-13)

The angel describes the life and responsibilities of their future son. (1:14-17)

Zechariah expresses doubt because of their ages. (1:18)

The angel answers, "I am Gabriel. I stand in the presence of God and have been sent to bring you this good news. Because you did not believe my words you will be silent until they come to pass." (1:19-20)

Elizabeth became pregnant and for five months remained in seclusion. She says, "The Lord has done this for me and removed my disgrace." (1:24-25)

Mary visits the home of Elizabeth and Zechariah. When Elizabeth hears the greeting of Mary, her child leaps within her womb and she is filled with the Holy Spirit. (1:39-44)

Elizabeth delivers a boy, and on the eighth day the circumcision and naming are arranged. Elizabeth declares his name is to be John. Her neighbors and relatives protest, "There is no one named John in your family." (1:57-60)

Zechariah writes "His name is to be John," then he regains his voice. Their neighbors and people of the town are amazed and wonder what this child will be? (1:61-66)

[Handwritten notes at top: "Asher - one of Israel's 12 Tribes in the Time of Moses. Promised a life blessed with abundance. Gen 30:23; Num 26:44-45"]

Study Questions

1. Zechariah emerges from the temple all excited and unable to speak. He rushes to Elizabeth with crazy flittering hand signals and rubs her abdomen. What do you think she is wondering at this point? Could she be thinking "Surely he has bumped his head or sniffed too much incense?"

2. Both Zechariah and Elizabeth are beyond child bearing age (Lu 1:7), but suddenly Zechariah is very interested in new attempts. How much do you think she is afraid of rekindling her hopes? If you counsel a young woman incapable of conceiving, what do you tell her regarding hope and prayer?

3. Visions in the temple don't happen every day, so once Elizabeth and her husband are back home, neighbors, friends, and relatives keep showing up at their door to hear about the vision. Explain the balance she faces in sharing the vision and not over- or under-stating the prophecy while her heart pounds with hope?

4. Elizabeth has her hopes for a child dashed every month for years. Now, due to her husband's inability to speak, how much will her faith increase?

5. Read Lu 1:41 – 45. How did Elizabeth know Mary was, "The mother of her Lord?" How did Elizabeth even know Mary was pregnant?

6. Cast your imagination into the moment when Elizabeth asks her husband, "What did the angel Gabriel look like?" Could she comprehend, "Glowing", or "Translucent"? Read Hebrews 13:2 Have you ever felt like you've come into contact with an angel? How do you describe it?

_____

_____

_____

7. The angel Gabriel told Zechariah that their child would be filled with the Holy Spirit even in the womb, Lu 1:15. Considering the rarity of such encounters prior to the arrival of Jesus, how would Elizabeth picture what that would be like?

_____

_____

_____

8. When Elizabeth realized she was pregnant, she went into seclusion for five months, Lu 1:24. Why do you think she did this?

_____

_____

_____

9. The prophecy about John, Lu 1:14-17, said he would be great in the sight of the Lord and go on in the spirit of Elijah. Expecting that God would watch her every day, how much courage do you believe Elizabeth needed to be the mother, guide, instructor, and example for this child?

_____

_____

_____

10. Elizabeth's husband Zechariah could not speak and probably could not hear. Turn to the person next to you and tell them 'your cow is stuck in a ditch' using only hand signals. Now, close your eyes to imitate the dark of night and using only touch, tell the person on your other side you think someone is at the door knocking? Do you now appreciate Elizabeth's sudden new challenge?

_____

_____

_____

Lessons

1. Be flexible. Elizabeth no longer held high hope for motherhood because of her age. God surprised her. When you offer your life to God, to let Him lead, to use you for His plans, be ready to adjust to new situations on short notice, or no notice. God will surprise you with people who help, prayers that are exceeded, miracles unexpected, and routines overturned. You will at times walk with majesty, witness angelic intercession, face turmoil with confidence, throw caution to the wind, kick out demons, get goose bumps and leap with joy. God sometimes shakes things up, to make conditions better, and uses us to do it.
2. Never let go of trust, faith, and hope. God is faithful, on the job, omniscient, and always motivated by love for us. When Elizabeth was a few months along in her pregnancy she said, "The Lord has done this for me and taken away my disgrace." (Lu 1:25)
3. Believe in yourself, God does. He knows your limits and your abilities. He will hand you the task and the ability in combination. God certainly knew Elizabeth was willing, strong, and committed, but could use a blessing of the Holy Spirit. She was fully willing to accept and follow God's plan even though she was new to the idea of raising a son with the standards required of a Nazarene.

Imagine That

1. Elizabeth goes into seclusion for five months. Is it because she wants to be certain of carrying the baby to full term before raising the expectations of those around her? Or, she wants to protect herself from stress during the first few months when baby growth is fragile and most at risk?
2. She must learn to communicate with Zechariah in new ways for several months, both, because he is frustrated with his silence, and because, at night she won't be able to hear him or see his gestures.
3. She must be patient as her husband tries to revisit and describe the events in the temple. The Angel said, "You are going to have a son."
4. Zechariah is again treating their intimate sex with anticipation and enthusiasm. She may have to overcome some suspicion and doubt. They are both very old and she knows well their history of attempts and failures to conceive. Yet, their hope is boosted as they recall testimony of Sarah and Abraham who could not conceive until God intervened.
5. People made signs to Zechariah (Lu 1:62). Is it possible he also couldn't hear so they had to use gestures? If so, Elizabeth would have to make sure he was looking at her when she wanted to communicate. That means she couldn't call him and would have to go looking for him every time she needed to share with him.
6. She learns the plan for the care of her son matches that of a Nazarene such as the restrictions and specifics for the rearing of Samson and Samuel. There are requirements and boundaries she must learn and abide by.
7. She will try to comprehend the weight of "He will go on before the Lord in the spirit and power of Elijah" (Lu 1:17). Her son will have the power of Elijah! He

was the prophet highly regarded by God, who defeated the 400 prophets of Baal on Mount Carmel (1 Kings 18). Her son will be a strong, positive force for God.
8. Even as the wife of a priest she bore the shame of barrenness, possibly implying the anger or displeasure of God (Lu 1:25). Now she can lift her head and laugh.
9. The Holy Spirit, through Elizabeth, expressed a grand truth and blessing, and did so in a loud voice. "Mary, you will be celebrated by all generations" (Lu 1:42).
10. Elizabeth remains loyal; "His name is to be John" (Lu 1:60). Surprising those near her to ask why; "There is no one in your family with that name."
11. Once Zechariah could speak again, he might run on continuously with joy, or be in the habit of silence. Did Elizabeth sometimes wish he would be quiet again, or forevermore enjoy the sound of his voice?

A Short Narrative

Mary and Elizabeth sit together on a hillside in the shade of an olive tree, relishing a gentle breeze during the hot afternoon. They share the wonder and blessings both are entering into, surprise motherhood. Elizabeth, who is in her sixth month of pregnancy, wears the obvious aspects of many new physical changes. Mary notices her timid movements, uneasy steps, persistent fatigue, labored breathing, and also, her unwavering smile. Elizabeth has not experienced this before and her apprehension shows in her timid eyes and trembling hands. However, she so yearned for this blessing that she bursts with the excitement that bolsters every other breath.

Mary just arrived yesterday to visit and already she has a thousand questions for Elizabeth. Mary watches her relative and inwardly speculates about her own experience just now beginning. What will she feel and look like, and is she worthy of the challenge?

Mary and Elizabeth share a bond created by God. Both are miraculously with child. Elizabeth, now too old to sustain a strong hope for this blessing, just yesterday felt the child in her womb leap with joy when Mary spoke her greeting. Mary aches to talk, almost non-stop, with anyone who will let her and not judge her. The faces of everyone who know she is pregnant betray their alarm, because they believe she violated the laws of God. Elizabeth is her best ally; herself recently, richly, walking in a miracle all day every day, positively accepts Mary's miraculous pregnancy as beautiful and as certain as the sunrise. Let's listen in.

Mary, "Tell me what this is like? Are you afraid? I see that you move with gentle steps, is it hard to do? Are you hoping for a boy or girl? Tell me tell me, I am erupting in excitement. I can't eat or sleep and can barely breathe."

Elizabeth, "They say a day is like a thousand years for God. Well He should see how long nine months is to a pregnant woman. It had to be a woman who established the word "Eternity". Some days I crave foods I could never tolerate before and then, just the opposite of that, there are some I usually loved until now. And, there are some which are now off limits like raisin cakes. Ooof! Gas and pregnancy are a bad combination." "Some anxious thoughts about my age and ability creep in, but I quickly remember how much I trust God and I know this is His plan for me."

Mary, "And, boy or girl?"

Elizabeth, "The angel Gabriel told Zechariah I would bring a son into the world. At my age, I am extremely happy with either boy or girl."

Mary, "Wow, an angel. I expect you can't get a more reliable prediction than that. I've come to trust them completely myself. Speaking of Zechariah, I haven't heard him say a word since I arrived. He stares and grumbles. Is he okay?"

Elizabeth laughs and squeezes Mary's hand. Have you not heard? Zechariah has not been able to speak or hear since the visit from the angel in the temple. We gradually learned that Zechariah expressed some doubt about the angel's announcement. So, the angel took his voice and hearing until the birth of our son is fulfilled."

Mary, "I bet that is exasperating."

Elizabeth, "Oh, much more than I ever imagined." Sighing, "All the simple communication we took for granted. Easy discussions, requests, explanations, compliments, and emotions are now a slow combination of writing, gestures, hand signals, and pointing. Sharing something as routine as plans for tomorrow exhausts both of us. Neither of us can just call out to the other with a question. We have to go find each other, whether inside or outside, and get their attention, and try not to startle each other with our sudden presence. I scare him a lot more than he scares me."

Mary, "I don't know how I would do it."

Elizabeth, "We have to watch each other's expressions closely to understand clearly. And well, it is actually making us closer and strengthening our love for each other. We groan a lot and laugh a lot. The biggest challenge is the night time. When either of us needs or wants to talk, one of us must light a candle, wake the other, and start the show. Just a week ago Zechariah had a nightmare about high winds damaging our crops. He woke up very anxious and began pulling and grabbing me and moaning loudly. He paced rapidly about in the dark, stubbing toes, knocking this and that over, and grunting. I couldn't get a candle lit fast enough before he ran outside in the dark. His pounding around woke the neighbors who had to tackle him to calm him down. Now the whole village gathers to share ideas about how to better communicate with him.

We didn't realize how many different meanings can be attached to some gestures and hand signals. There were thirty of us having to mesh and learn five new fabricated languages overnight. Our neighbor was trying to say our cow got out and Zechariah thought he was signaling his fence has four legs. One other confusing event bothered Zechariah. A man near our corral was motioning with his thumb, nose, and cheeks and we were not sure if we had a new baby pig or our dog was ugly. This is how some great humor came to our village. With a flurry of hand waves a man said, "I did not signal, 'Your mother rides a camel to work.' I meant she makes nice blankets for their backs." We laugh a lot more these days. We still aren't sure about the difference between, 'Where do we feed the camels?' and 'Go get the water yourself'."

Mary, "And how are you holding up with the double challenge of new pregnancy and non speaking husband?"

Elizabeth, "We get aggravated, so we hold each other often for reassurance. I miss his voice a lot. He would whisper I love you in my ear. Now he blows in my ear instead, which is kind of nice too, once I get past the goose bumps. You asked me if I was afraid. In some ways, I am. Not to bear a child, for I trust God to help. I am not afraid to be a parent and guardian. But, we are not going to just teach this child the proper qualities of life, respect, honesty, diligent work, and such. No, we have to prepare him to face and carry out the task of being the voice of God and declaring the importance of the arrival of God. Who knows what we will need, to be able to train our son for that responsibility?

He is to live a Holy life even from birth and will have restrictions on every day activities like his food and drink."

Mary, "Be brave and strong, and take every step hand in hand with God; His love endures forever" (Psalm 136).

Conclusion

Elizabeth knows and loves God, and her husband is a priest. These two facts are in contrast with, and fail to explain, why she is denied the joy she seeks, motherhood. Barrenness causes her disgrace, bewilderment, and humility. Still, she trusts God. Her pregnancy replaces her disappointment with extreme joy, but she proceeds cautiously. She goes into seclusion for five months possibly to avoid the intense emotional agony and public humiliation if the pregnancy fails. While she is gradually becoming pretty certain of carrying to full term, she cherishes the visit of her relative Mary. Now, the anticipation of what the angel said her son will present to the world invades her thoughts every day. Her child would be raised similar to Samson as a Nazarene, dedicated to God. Samson's parents prayed for help to know how to raise Samson (Judges 13:8). Elizabeth now bravely faces the duty of raising a child to be used by God. She thinks, "God will be watching my every move, hearing everything I say to John, guiding and encouraging me along the way." "I can't do it alone, but with God's help, and Zechariah's help, I can do it." She is zealous. Imagine her courage. We know she succeeded because we get to see into her future, our past, John the Baptist declaring to all of us, "Repent, and be baptized." (Lu 3:3-11)

Esther

Introduction – 478 BC

Esther and her cousin Mordecai are exiles, foreigners in a land not their own. They possess no power or wealth, but together, they make history the Jews honor every year. This is the story of two Queens, two Knights, and a King. If the story wasn't in the Bible we might easily believe Shakespeare wrote it. It involves great moments of drama, deception, rage, fear, revenge, humility, and power. We feel the dread, and the eventual defeat, of the villain. We drink in the beauty of two queens, conspire with the commoner Mordecai to prod the king to mercy, tremble with Esther as she requests a moment of the king's time, and finally, we cheer the triumph of justice. Esther risks her own life and the end result is the rescue of her nation. The enduring symbol of their victory is Purim, the national annual celebration that today, 2500 years later, is still observed and cherished throughout Jewish communities all around the world. Additionally, the King gave the Jews permission to plunder their enemies possessions, but they did not (Est 9:10, 15, & 16). This fact reflects positively on the integrity of the nation.

In the year 586 BC the city of Jerusalem was captured and the Israelites were exiled to Babylon, several hundred miles to the east of their homeland. One hundred years later, when Persia held most of the land north of Israel, King Xerxes came to power. He loved to flaunt his wealth and his wife, Queen Vashti. When she resisted this parade of her beauty, the king removed her from her position of prestige, and that opened the door for her replacement. Esther's tale is a chronicle of her journey from a humble beginning, then along a fairytale path all the way to the throne as Queen. It is a robust adventure, so hang on tight.

Bible account in the book of Esther

King Xerxes is really pleased with himself. So, he puts his possessions on display for all his officials to come admire. He also gives a banquet that lasts seven days. On the last day he makes a decision filtered through a pool of too much alcohol and decides to put his queen on display. She refuses to participate and that angers the king. (1:1-12)

King Xerxes consults with his advisors and a decree is issued to remove Queen Vashti from the king's presence and take her title away. (1:13-22)

In order to replace Queen Vashti a collection of beautiful, eligible women was added to the king's harem. Esther was one of them and she was exceptional. She was assigned seven female attendants and treated for a year with oils and perfumes and with the best foods. Everyone placed her in a position of most favored, including the king. Esther is now Queen Esther, and a banquet is held in her honor. (2:1-18)

Esther's cousin Mordecai overhears a conspiracy to kill the king, reports the plot, and saves the king's life. God tucks this event away for future use, in chapter six. (2:19-23)

The Bible introduces us to Haman, whom King Xerxes honors by promoting him to the second highest seat in the realm. All citizens are commanded to bow to Haman, but Mordecai refuses. Haman is furious beyond just everyday rage. (3:1-6)

Haman seeks the death of Mordecai for certain, but his anger extends to killing off all of Mordecai's people, the Jews, as well. Haman forms a plan to slaughter all the Jews in the kingdom and with the help of the "Pur", he forecasts a date for their execution. King Xerxes, still honoring Haman and not realizing the plan will include the death of Esther, grants Haman's request and allows the decree to be issued. (3:7-15)

Mordecai learns about the plan to execute all Jews and so he makes a big show of anguish in public. When Queen Esther sends messengers to console him, he requests she approach the king to protect her people. (4:1-8)

Esther resists the request to impose upon the king, but Mordecai reminds her of two issues. One, she too is a Jew possibly subject to the execution decree, and two, maybe she is placed near the king for this very reason. Esther replies "Have all the Jews in Susa fast for three days and I will do the same. Then I will approach the king." (4:9-16)

Esther risks her life to see the king, and then invites him to a banquet. She also invites Haman whose pride prevents him from realizing the trap she is setting. When the king asks her to reveal her request, she asks for protection from the decree that will kill her and her people. Only when the king asks "Who did this?" does Esther point out Haman. (5:1-8, 7:1-10)

Esther pleads with the king for relief from the decree that cannot be retracted. The king issues a new decree permitting the Jews to defend themselves against all attacks. (8:3-11)

Esther's efforts result in the salvation of a nation and are remembered every year as a national celebration called "Purim". (9:20-28)

Study Questions

StaR

1. Chapter two. Esther lives in a nation not her own. She has lost and learned to live without her parents. Now she is taken to be scrutinized as a potential for the position of Queen of a nation. At the last minute, her cousin Mordecai tells her to conceal her nationality. Describe her sleepless nights. What is it like to have to guard your identity? How do you calm your nerves knowing you face the demands of exaltation as Queen, or the shame of rejection?

   silent Save Nation Brave
   Pressure — Robe of who you are!

2. There is something suspicious afoot and we get the hint in Est 2:14. The candidates who have spent the night with the king are not allowed to return and be with the waiting candidates. What does that tell Esther?

3. Esther was enhanced with twelve months of beauty treatments before she was taken in to be with the king. It included six months with oils and six with perfumes and cosmetics and she had seven attendants applying them, Est 2:9 & 12. Never again will I ask, "What takes a woman so long in the bathroom?" How much patience for this process, and courage for the anticipation of the approaching unknown, do you think this required of Esther?

4. Esther, like everyone in the kingdom, knows how easily Queen Vashti was deposed and disposed. When the virgins were assembled a second time (Est 2:19), how much anxiety does this cause her as the new Queen?

5. There are no references to "God" or "Lord" in the book of Esther and no direct dialogues with either, so in your opinion, why is this book in the Bible? Even so, argue the point that divine intervention is involved in the Book of Esther. Use one of the following paragraphs: Est 2:17-18, 21-23, 5:1-3, or 6:1-11.

___

6. Boast about Esther's integrity from her dialogue with the king in chapter 5:1-8.

___

7. Identify and rate the courage of Esther from her warning in 4:9 – 11 and her actions in 4:15 - 5:2. Why do you give her this rating?

___

8. Esther sent a message to Mordecai asking all the Jews in Susa to fast, and stating she would do the same (4:16). What was her purpose for this mortification? Explain the psychology behind Ezra 8:21.

___

9. Proverbs 16:18 says, "Pride goes before destruction…" How did this truth work in the hands of Esther to trap Haman? (5:9 – 14 & 7:1 – 6)

___

10. Esther shifts from timid (4:15 – 16) to ruthless (9:13). What do you see as the primary cause in this change?

___

Lessons

1. Mordecai told Esther that she could participate in God's plan or keep silent. If she chose to keep silent, God would use someone else, and His plan would proceed. It is the same for us. If we give ourselves to God he will use us. If He comes to us to participate and we stall, he will proceed with someone else, and we will miss the joy of working with God.
2. Fasting was vital to Esther and should be a part of our walk with God. In the book of Esther, the practice of fasting appears twice. In 4:3 Mordecai fasted to protest the king's decree for extermination of all Jews. In 4:16, Esther fasted before she approached the king to stop the extermination. The next few points, 3 – 8, about fasting should be noted.
3. In Ezra 8:21 a fast is called for to, "humble ourselves before God". That was the primary purpose for them and it is the same for us.
4. In Judges 20:26 the Israelites fasted before entering into a battle. They were seeking the approval and help of God.
5. In 2 Samuel 12:15-16 David fasted and lay in sackcloth while his son was ill and might die. David was hopeful but not successful.
6. Both David and Mordecai clothed themselves in sackcloth while they fasted. Fasting is internal mortification and sackcloth is one external visible symbol of our prostration. Self humiliation is the purpose. Esther could not wear sackcloth even if she wanted to, because it was forbidden in the palace.
7. Jesus said, "When you fast, do not distort your face as the hypocrites do. Wash your face so no one will know" (Mt 6:16&17). It is between you and God, so don't seek the sympathy of the people around you. Mordecai went about town in sackcloth and wailing. David lay on the floor in sackcloth and fasted. Both of them made it very obvious they were suffering in their appeal to God. But today, Jesus tells us the outward show is not for us to put on. He says God will see what is done in secret and reward our dedication to Him.
8. Jesus said, "When you fast…" not "If you fast…" This implies fasting should be a regular occurrence in our lives with instances and frequencies selected to increase our walk with God.
9. Esther held the title of Queen, and still approached the king with respect and humility. We should make that our mandate. Whether we undertake simple matters, or those of grand importance, approach others with the best demonstration of respect we can display. Leave any form of self importance at home and advance meekly. Remember what Jesus told us, "The greatest among you will be your servant. For those who exalt themselves, will be humbled, and those who humble themselves, will be exalted." (Mt 23:11&12)

Imagine That

1. Esther is raised with awareness of circumstances that tug hard at her heart. She is a foreigner in a land distant from her heritage. She is raised by her cousin because both of her parents died. We hope Esther knew them for some number of years before Mordecai "took her as his own daughter when her parents died." (2:7)

2. Esther never set foot in her homeland and yet caused the celebration and holiday, called Purim, her fellow Israelites still honor 2500 years after the event she started. She is remembered every year for risking her life to save her nation.
3. She set the stage for the downfall of Haman. Because her first banquet proceeded with no negative result, both King Xerxes and Haman dropped their guard during the second banquet. By having Haman present when she informs the king about Haman's evil scheme, King Xerxes can immediately witness the shock and panic on Haman's face. This certainly confirmed what Esther was reporting.

A Short Narrative

Esther's life journey is landmarked with traumatic family adversity and with turning points created by random, rash, or risky decrees, edicts, or proclamations. Early on she is raised by her cousin Mordecai after she loses both of her parents. She and Mordecai are in exile to Babylon and disconnected from tradition and the prominent cultural ways of her homeland.

Turning point number one. Cacophony resounds in scores of town squares. Troops and horses pound and strut, kicking up thick dust that clouds the air. Frantic voices call out. Some citizens approach while others scatter and hide. Suddenly the air is vibrating with the blast of a loud trumpet and the bellow of the Herald, "Hear ye, hear ye, all loyal subjects to King Xerxes. Let it be known in all 127 provinces that today, in the citadel of Susa, Queen Vashti has forfeited the crown. Whilst disrespectfully refusing the king's request for her public appearance she has lost all authority, majesty, and honor in the eyes of the king and his nobles. Therefore, she is henceforth denied access to King Xerxes and all royal particulars of the throne. This declaration is forever irrevocable.

The edict is hammered to the town's gate with flourish, and before the herald mounts his steed, the rumors, gasps, whispers, and rustlings charge the air. "Where will she go? Will the king vent his anger on the little towns? Are we safe? Will our taxes increase?" The elders of the town call out for calm and retrieve the edict. Again, slowly the edict is read to the folks gathered in the square. "Fellow citizens, do not be alarmed. This is too far removed from our village to cause us concern. Please go about your daily progress and give this no further consideration. It is not for us to hinder our peace or tranquility."

In time, seasons and affairs advance.

Turning point number two. Once again the king's troops are making a ruckus in town, usually a bad sign, but this seems different. Suddenly the air is vibrating with the blast of a loud trumpet and the bellow of the Herald, "Hear ye, hear ye, all loyal subjects to King Xerxes. Let it be known in all 127 provinces that today, in the citadel of Susa, a decree is issued and in earnest throughout the realm a search now commences for all fair maidens to appear for evaluation and recommendation to assume the role vacated by Vashti. We now seek the best in our noble land to become the next queen of the realm. Know it sure and well, to be considered is the highest of honors, to be chosen exceeds the dreams of the stars. Prompt yourselves to promote your finest of ladies for this one-time event."

Multiple copies of the decree, in multiple languages, are hammered with enhanced flourish, to gates, wagons, doorposts, and benches in the square. This is big news.

Nationwide maidens jostle, tickle, tease, and encourage each other with hopes and doubts regarding this looming fantasy. "Hurry up, clear the way, read it again, do you think I should?" Wardrobes are scrutinized, faces washed, bets made, prayers said, coins counted, winks shared, hugs traded, and witticisms bantered. The frenzy ripples across the country and several times caresses the ears of Esther. In the citadel of Susa, the lines form and lengthen, but Esther excels, shines, is chosen, and is elevated to the status of Queen Esther. The king is elated.

In time, seasons and affairs advance.

<u>Turning point number three</u>. Esther's cousin, Mordecai offends Haman, one of King Xerxes nobles. Haman can hardly contain himself and he would have called for Mordecai's head right there but a sinister plan hatches in his imagination. He tricks King Xerxes into authorizing a nationwide extermination of all Jews.

The king's troops ride into town more urgently now. There is a grim feeling about the scowl visible on their faces. Suddenly the air is vibrating with the blast of a loud trumpet and the bellow of the Herald, "Hear ye, hear ye, all loyal subjects to King Xerxes. Let it be known in all 127 provinces that today, in the citadel of Susa, the king issued a decree setting a date for total destruction of all Jews residing within the realm. The date proclaimed is the thirteenth day of the twelfth month. On that day kill all the Jews, young and old, male and female, and take their possessions." This event is planned and proclaimed more than half a year in advance. Perpetrators and potential victims as well, know it is coming. There is plenty of time to prepare on both sides.

<u>Turning point number four</u>. Mordecai protests the planned extermination very loudly in the streets. He covers himself in sackcloth and ashes. When Esther learns why, Mordecai pushes her to approach the king in behalf of all Jews.

Mordecai: "Esther, You must go to the king and get him to remove this decree. Our people will perish if we do nothing."

Esther: "No, no, this is not good. Do you not know his vow on this? No one is allowed to just show up to see the king. It is annoying to him and he has annoying people killed." "However, I haven't been called in to the king in the last 30 days. Perhaps I will be soon, and then going to the king may not annoy him and lead to my death."

Mordecai: "The risk carries the value, in the eyes of the king, and in the eyes of God. It could be God's plan that put you there for just this moment."

Esther responds: "Very well. Have the Jews in Susa fast in preparation for three days and I will go to the king. To remind the king of her value to him, she puts on her royal robe and then stands patiently in the inner court waiting. Now, let's pause in our story here for a minute to note. We in the 21st century, with multiple Bible translations, can relax. We know she succeeds, we know her effort gave birth to the annual victory celebration called Purim that the Jews cherish every year since. We aren't tense for her anymore. But let's insert ourselves into the story, and stand beside her in the inner court. Esther is recalling the reports of many people who ventured this far and failed. She waits and listens to muffled conversations and she is watchful for promising signs from the nobles and throne. Under that luxurious royal robe her two knees are a knocking. Her adrenaline rushes to every nerve as she silently rehearses her appeal. She weighs the value of her past with him and the value of her people. Esther is praying hard and God stands there with her. It is His people she represents. He smiles at her trembling hands and blows warmly on them.

Esther's appeal to the king is victorious. Suddenly, in all the towns, the air is vibrating with the blast of a loud trumpet and the bellow of the Herald, "Hear ye, Hear ye, all loyal subjects to King Xerxes. Let it be known in all 127 provinces that today, in the citadel of Susa, the king issued a decree for all Jews to be brave and stand together. Since no royal decree can be revoked, a new decree is set to balance the scale. On the thirteenth day of the twelfth month, if any aggression against the Jews should occur, the Jews have full permission of the king to defend themselves.

Esther rejoices; her nation is protected. Most of their opponents turn cowardly, not wanting an actual fight. The Israelites can defend themselves, but they do not plunder. Their safety is assured and the integrity of the nation is not tarnished.

Conclusion regarding Queen Esther

Imagine her loyalty. She followed the directions of Mordecai even after she became queen, a certain position of some authority to do as she pleased.

Imagine her fear. She knew three things concerning her royal position. First, she knew how easily the king could replace a queen after Vashti was dethroned. Second, she knew how often the king requested her presence; a lapse of thirty days isn't a strong reinforcement assuring her enduring presence. Third, she knew virgins were again being brought before the king, which was the process by which she replaced Queen Vashti. These issues combined reminded her of her precarious survival in the kingdom. It is frightening to know you could be deposed and disposed of so easily.

Imagine her courage. She knew her life could be terminated quite simply and quickly if she inappropriately approached the king and was rejected. She gave careful consideration, prepared appropriately, sought the approval of God, and stood firm in the king's court, with knees knocking and pulse pounding. She employed those deep breathing exercises she saw the eunuchs practicing. Esther was very brave and countless descendants of Israel owe their existence to her.

Eve

Introduction – Day 6

Adam named his wife Eve because she would become the mother of all the living. (Genesis 3:20) Eve was the first woman, first wife, and first mother. Each of those roles she filled with the purest honesty any woman ever presented. She filled them all naturally from her heart, with no examples to imitate. Absolute innocence drove her every action, thought and word. She talked to God face to face and knew the sound of His voice. She leisurely strolled in a flawless garden and daily tasted fruit created as an absolute perfect fit for a human. She knew mystery, joy, accomplishment, surprise, excitement, marvel, fond memories, and happiness. Eve lived without fear or stress, for awhile.

Then, she disobeyed God and felt His disappointment and anger. She watched the arrival of decay and death, and felt new feelings of apprehension, disappointment, grief, regret, and pain. She felt the shock and shame of perfect majestic beauty losing life all around her.

A lot of people place the blame on Eve for everything in the world going wrong. But if that is the extent of our evaluation regarding Eve, we easily bypass and unfortunately overlook the depth and treasure of her maternal intuition and guidance. Yes, she did disobey God, but on the positive side, she also left us with words of wisdom we should earnestly apply all our life. In her dialogue with the serpent, she told us one of the simplest most effective ways to resist temptation and vanquish the devils schemes. In a few simple, subtle words, she gave us a powerful shield to use for our own protection. Did you see them? They are presented here in the section on lessons.

Bible account of Eve in Genesis chapters one through four.

No suitable helper for Adam was found among the animals God made, so God formed a woman from one of Adam's ribs. (2:18-22)

God created Adam and Eve and gave them authority over all the animals. He also gave them all seed bearing plants and fruit for food. (1:27-29)

Adam was told he could eat from any tree in the garden except the tree of knowledge of good and evil, because if he did, he would die. (2:16-17)

Eve was deceived and disobeyed God's command by eating the forbidden fruit and giving some to Adam. Suddenly they knew the difference between good and evil and could not return to pure innocence. (3:1-6)

God learned of their disobedience and since this was the very first time a human disobeyed Him, He was pretty angry. He said, "What is this you have done?" to Eve. (3:11-13)

Then God penalized them with a curse. For the man, exhausting labor would fill his life. For the woman, painful childbirth would rise up to meet her. (3:16-19)

God banished them from the garden forever. (3:23)

Adam and Eve became parents with the births of Cain and Abel. (4:1-2)

Cain kills Abel. God sends Cain away to be a restless wanderer. (4:8-12)

God grants Eve another son and Eve rejoices over the birth of Seth. (4:25)

Study Questions

1. Adam lived 930 years. How long did Eve live?
   a. 797   b. 814   c. 931   (d.) We don't know

2. How many children did Adam and Eve have?
   a. 3   b. 5   c. 7   d. We don't know

3. What were the three progressive steps in Eve's downfall? Ge 3:6

4. Describe situations where you have witnessed those three steps personally?

5. There are two other actions taken by Eve which we should identify and avoid. One occurred before she looked at the fruit and the other one occurred after she took the fruit. Can you locate and explain each? Ge 3:4 – 6

6. Committing a sin involves a series of steps. Where in the process do we have the best chance of resistance and victory?

7. How well prepared was Eve to face the deceptions of Satan? How well prepared are we and how can we improve it?

8. Compare Ge 2:17 with Ge 3:3. When Eve answered the serpent, why do you think she modified the original commandment from God?

9. Determine and describe why you think her change to the original commandment hurts or helps us.

10. Eve experienced several emotionally traumatic issues. First, she angered God. Second, she and Adam were evicted from the garden. Third, she lost her only children, Cain and Abel, through bad misfortune. Do you believe it is natural for a woman to turn away from God when she suffers trauma or loss? How would you help her return to God with faith?

Lessons from Eve

1. Genesis 3:6 describes the stages Eve went through that led to her downfall. This explanation provides us with great insight and guidance because we face the exact same course every time we choose to disobey God. Here is the verse about Eve's failure. "When the woman saw that the fruit of the tree was good for food and pleasing to the eye, and also desirable for gaining wisdom, she took some and ate." There are three steps here. First, she "saw", then she "justified" the choice, and then she "took" the fruit. That is the chain of events that lead to disaster. That is the chain we have to break. So where is the link in the chain we can break? In some situations we can prevent the stage of seeing a temptation, but the second stage is easier to predict and break. That is where we spend time trying to rationalize why the choice is a good idea. That was where Eve was noticing the fruit was pleasing to the eye and desirable for gaining wisdom. Think about our own moments where we tell ourselves "One time won't hurt," or "I'll do better tomorrow." Those and a hundred others are the arguments we offer to allow ourselves to think the disobedience is okay. Instead, as soon as we recognize the temptation, immediately change your thinking to subjects that you can invite God to share. Eve wasn't the only Bible character to describe this process. In Joshua 7:21 Achan reports that he "saw" a robe and some silver, he "coveted them" and "took" them. The process does not occur so fast that it can overwhelm us. As soon as you see, turn away. James 1:15 says, "… each person is tempted when they are dragged away by their own desire."

2. Eve was wise and gave us four of the most powerful words of advice we could ever ask for. This is her gift to us as I mentioned in the last line of the Introduction of Eve. Her advice is so important that it should not be read near any distractions or in a hurry. It is unfortunate that she is sometimes derided for saying this before people notice how precious it is for us. We must praise God for sharing it, honor Eve for saying it, and thank Moses for writing it down. It is so valuable that I write her words here, without paraphrase, from three Bible versions, King James, New American Standard, and The New International Version. In comparison, there is an important difference between God's command to Adam, and Eve repeating that command as a response to the serpent's challenge.

God said to Adam – Genesis 2:16-17

King James. "And the Lord God commanded the man, saying, 'Of every tree of the garden thou mayest eat; But of the tree of the knowledge of good and evil, thou shalt not eat of it; for in the day that thou eatest thereof thou shalt surely die'."

New American Standard. "And the Lord God commanded the man, saying 'From any tree of the garden you may eat freely; but from the tree of the knowledge of good and evil you shall not eat, for in the day that you eat from it you shall surely die'."

New International Version. "And the Lord God commanded the man, 'You are free to eat from any tree in the garden; but you must not eat from the tree of the knowledge of good and evil, for when you eat from it you will certainly die'."

Now, notice how Eve shares that command with the serpent – Genesis 3:2-3

King James. "And the woman said unto the serpent, 'We may eat of the fruit of the trees of the garden; But of the fruit of the tree which is in the midst of the garden, God hath said,' 'Ye shall not eat of it, neither shall ye touch it, lest ye die'."

New American Standard. "And the woman said to the serpent, 'From the fruit of the trees of the garden we may eat; but from the fruit of the tree which is in the middle of the garden, God has said,' 'You shall not eat from it or touch it, lest you die'."

New International Version. "The woman said to the serpent, 'We may eat fruit from the trees in the garden, but God did say,' 'You must not eat fruit from the tree that is in the middle of the garden, and you must not touch it, or you will die'."

It is easy to spot the difference between God's command to Adam, and Eve's response to the serpent. Eve added, "You must not touch it" to the original command. I have heard people say her addition is just one more of her mistakes. Perhaps, but I think we are too hasty if we accept that view and quit there. God allowed her words to be in the Bible or, wanted them to be there for us, Moses wrote them down for us, and nowhere in the Bible is Eve charged with error for adding them.

So, can we gain anything from what she said? Yes! It is an enormous advantage for us, a tool we can employ to help us resist temptation. There is a subtle barrier between us and each temptation and because God won't tempt us, it is we who breach the barrier and reach for the item we shouldn't touch. Consider the variety of ways we come into contact with, or "touch" those items. "Touching it" can be converted to any one of our five senses. For example, we can taste alcohol, smell cigarettes, hear vulgar or abusive language or music, see scantily clad people, or feel the touch of someone not your spouse. These issues may come between a person and their relationship with God. Deciding ahead of the arrival of temptation that we will not even "touch" the article will help ensure we maintain resistance.

Let's take a look at a few possible situations where this can be applied. For instance, if alcohol is our weakness, it is easier to resist if we are not holding it. The devil will find someone to hand you a beer. So, put distance between ourselves and the alcohol. Don't have it in the house, don't go where it is being served, don't attend gatherings where it is abundant. Don't even touch it. If you must be near it, fill your hand with tea, coffee, or soda. Any barrier is better than none.

If your weakness is pornography, in what ways can you apply "Don't touch it?" Well since you know where it is, stay away from those locations. Avoid the book stores, magazine racks, and an endless supply of web sites. Don't go near the magazine racks. Don't visit the internet websites. Steer clear of that section of the book store. As soon as it is in your hand, as soon as you open the website, your resistance is diminished.

What if your downfall is gambling? Again, you know where it is, the casinos, website games for money, scratch cards at convenience stores, and others. Application of Eve's "Don't even touch it" plan would best be served by completely avoiding casinos and websites. They are designed to draw you in with bells, and lights, and in many casinos, free drinks. Eve would say, "Don't increase your risk" of failure. Do not touch.

If I struggle with gossip, anger, or depression, stay away from the situations that add to those challenges. Change or shorten the contact, walk away, introduce something positive into the moment.

If I struggle with weight problems and I am at a buffet, I can linger and stare at the deserts, or kick my feet along and move to the other end of the table and consider and TOUCH the fruit salad. What are my chances of resistance if I pick up a donut and intentionally, forcefully, and eagerly recall or imagine the taste?

This is a process of keeping aware of any situation that displeases God, and watching out for them. Let me add a special note here. Sometimes the items that come between us and God aren't the problem. The problem is we like ourselves less when we participate in them and when we like ourselves less we may have less confidence in walking with God. When we love ourselves less, we have less love for others, maybe even including God.

Notice how Eve's statement, "Do not even touch," could have worked for her. Her temptation is the forbidden fruit. If the fruit remains on the tree at a distance, the temptation is much easier to resist than if she approaches and touches the fruit. Touching the fruit removes one barrier and reduces the strength of her resistance. Genesis 3:6, tells us "she saw the fruit was good for food, pleasing to the eye, and desirable for gaining wisdom". At that moment she should have applied her own advice, but you know she took and ate. Pretty soon after, she may have thought, "If I just hadn't touched it."

Avoiding the subtle, but not so innocent, in-roads for temptation will continuously help us maintain strong resistance. Eve knew the hazard of 'contact' with the forbidden object. Her words, "Don't even touch it!" work to protect us if we apply them. Eve, we thank you. A humorous quote I heard runs like this, "Until I was four I thought my name was No No." Eve is standing right behind us, or inside our thoughts, and she is saying, "No No, don't touch that." Eve, we thank you.

Imagine That

1. Imagine Eve's courage. She faced a few challenges: a conversation with a serpent, an angry creator, and child birth. She knew childbirth was forecast as painful. Then when the pain began, there was no one to tell her how much it would increase and when it would end. Also, there were no pain reducers, except holding Adam's hand.
2. God said, "If you eat from this tree, you will surely "die". How did Adam and Eve define the word "die"? What image came to their thoughts when they pictured the word "die"? We are familiar with wrinkles and gray hair and walkers and hospital beds and funeral homes and open casket viewing and cemeteries. But Eve only knew plants and animals. Genesis 2:15 says God put the man in the garden to "… work it and take care of it". Plants and leaves wither and die, but it would be doubtful for Eve to think of that as an example of what dying might be to her. Did she see animals die before they were evicted from the garden? If so, would she think of them when she imagined what dying looked like. Animals are often pretty quiet about it. But when Adam and Eve ate the forbidden fruit, they didn't physically die, so they knew immediately that was not the definition of "die". With the whole Bible in our hands we understand that death is separation or disconnection from God. To Adam and Eve who were at one time in perfect harmony with God, even one minute of disconnection from God would feel worse than death.

3. Eve faced the unknown experience of childbirth with no human advisor. God said to her that He would greatly increase her pain in childbirth. Her only examples were the animals which she could watch delivering their young. But they rarely seemed to experience and show their pain during the process. Perhaps after delivering her first child Cain, she clearly thought, "Wow, I wish I had listened to God and not eaten the forbidden fruit. We share a similar position. There are hundreds of lines of great advice in the book of Proverbs that Bible readers may take lightly until they ignore one that later stings them. If only we listen to God and take the path He suggests, there would be a lot less pain in our lives.

4. Motherhood must have been an extreme mystery for Eve. She did not have another female to ask questions. She did not have a mother, or aunt, or sister who had been through it all and could advise her. She had the examples of animals which are certainly misleading if you use them as a guide. Then perhaps God gave her instruction and instinct, but merely hearing about a biological process is far different from actually participating in it.

5. Consider the difference between Eve's motherhood experiences and the animal examples visible around her every day. Most newborn animals are walking in just a few days, but Cain just lay there, even after six months of life he is only rolling over, sitting up, and crawling. Eve must have worried to Adam, "He doesn't walk." They are calling to God, "There is something wrong." God replies, "Patience my child, all things in their time." Adam and Eve could talk, but Cain just screamed, maybe laughed, but no words were spoken at first. When Cain did start to talk, maybe there wasn't a word "Mom" yet, and Cain heard Adam call Eve by name, so Cain called her Eve.

6. How old were Adam and Eve? Nothing about age appears until Genesis 5:3 where it says Adam was 130 years old when he fathered Seth. Maybe they weren't called years at first, but were referred to as seasons, which God designed as repeating markers of time. (Ge 1:14)

7. Eve was fully grown when she started aging, so imagine the possible humor in conversation. In a random season, when Abel was old enough to wonder, he might ask Eve, "How many seasons old are you?" Eve could answer, "I have been alive eight seasons." Abel would be confused and say, "If Cain and I are six and you are eight, how come Cain and I are so much smaller than you?" Of course I don't know their actual age differences, but the possibilities can give us fun, wow moments to consider.

8. Eve never experienced childhood. She appeared as an adult. So when Cain and Abel were busy being boys, she must have been very surprised. "What is all this yelling and running and throwing things? Why are they always so dirty and don't care?" Probably when Adam joined in with the jostling Eve needed to go down to the river for a swim. Then she had to wait over a hundred years to at last have a daughter. As her daughter grew perhaps she thought, "At last, a child with finesse."

9. Eve certainly experienced grief we are not told about; she loses both of her children in a very short time. As life teaches us, it is expected that children will bury their parents, but when the reverse occurs, it tears us apart. Parents are often inconsolable and beyond comforting when their child dies from illness or injury.

Consider Eve's situation as well. Her second son, Abel is murdered, and her first son, Cain, is sent away (Ge 4:8-12). These two events must have shocked Eve and overwhelmed her with grief. Now she and Adam are alone together again. What did God say to her? How did she get past the anguish? We don't know how long it persisted, but we can certainly imagine her joy when she gives birth to Seth. We may easily picture the very first "overprotective" mother, afraid of losing another child.

10. I believe the feeling of guilt followed Eve everywhere for many years. Certainly she realized the beauty all around her was unraveling and she at least suspected it was her fault. We do not know when or how God informed her about a way to be reconciled with Him. It would be more than two thousand years before Moses would write Leviticus chapter four describing blood sacrifice atonement for sinners. It would be another 1500 years before Paul and others would write about the sacrifice of Jesus to reconcile sinners with God. As soon as we choose to we can run to God, accept the sacrifice of Jesus for our redemption, and ask Him to be our Lord. We can find relief from our guilt any time we want. What did Eve do to get past her guilt? God loves all of us and doesn't want to lose even one. He rescued her, but the guilt still weighed on her heavily.

These are some of the background events I imagine as possible or probable in Eve's life. You may have several of your own. I'd like to hear them.

A Short Narrative

Adam is just waking up, there is a gentle breeze whooshing the nearby leaves around. Eve, lying beside him, has her ear on Adam's chest and she is awake but still and quiet.

Adam: "Eve. Eve! Eve!!!"

Eve: "Shush! I'm listening. There is something thumping inside you."

Adam: "I don't hear any thumping. What do you think it is?"

Eve: "I don't know. You may have broken something when you played with that lion yesterday. I first heard it while you were sleeping and I moved close to you. The thumping is quiet and constant. I can hear it and feel it if my cheek is on your chest."

Adam:, "Let me put my ear on your chest to hear if you have it too."

Eve: "Okay, put your ear right here."

Adam: "I hear it! I hear it! We both have it. It sounds like coconuts falling out of the trees, when they land on the path." "Eve, when you touch my hand the thumping goes faster."

Eve: "It does? My turn again. Shift over. Let me listen and then when I signal, hold my hand." "Okay, now!" Adam is still for a moment of silent pause. "Yes, I hear it. Now take my hand." They are still for another moment of quiet. "You're right, it goes faster. It must be a good thump because when we touch, it thumps quicker.

Adam: "I wonder if the animals have it too. I'm going to go listen to them."

Eve: "Yea, try getting them to hold still while you listen. Adam!! I want to talk with you about the animals."

Adam: "Okay, what is your concern?"

Eve: "What did you name that thing with the really long neck?"

Adam: "The camel?"

Eve: "No, taller."

Adam: "Giraffe?"

Eve: "Yes, that thing!"

Adam: "What about it?"

Eve: "It's eating all the pears from the top of the tree again."

Adam: "Well, we can't reach them anyway."

Eve: "But, eventually, left alone, they fall down to us. And another thing, the bears are eating all the blackberries before they're ripe. Just because you name all the animals, do they have to remain so near to us? There are plants with food in other places."

Adam: "You know, I think this pregnancy is making you short tempered."

Eve: "Well, it's hard to accept all these changes. I hurt everywhere and I used to love pomegranates and now they make me gag. I can't sleep at night or stay awake during the day. This is taking too long."

Adam: "God said it would only be 9 months."

Eve: "Well, I wish it was like the deer with only 6 months, or the dog, with only two months."

Adam: "Look on the bright side. It could be like the elephant with 21 months."

Eve: "Ugh! Have you watched one of them deliver? I'd never walk again. Do you think I'll have only one baby? I've seen cats deliver 4 at a time."

Adam: "Well, you only have two arms and two breasts. Perhaps that is a clue to ability."

Eve: "Okay, two would be a good start. I can manage two at a time."

Adam: "I notice you wear flowers in your hair. It looks very nice."

Eve: "They smell nice and make me feel better, maybe even reduce my headaches."

Adam: "The blue flowers match your eyes."

Eve: "Wait! What? My eyes are blue? You said my eyes are blue?"

Adam: "Yes, like the sky. You didn't know? See the green circle around the center of my eyes. Yours are blue, a little bit similar to the flowers you are wearing."

Eve: "How do you know your eyes are green?"

Adam: "From my reflection in the water at the river."

Eve: "I never see my reflection, the water moves too fast."

Adam: "Make a pool on the side. Come, I'll show you."

Grasping Eve's hand they race to the river. Adam digs into the bank below the water line and lets it fill. Then he makes a wall between the pool and the river.

Adam: "When the water motion settles down, you can see your reflection on the surface. In the morning, when the bright circle is low in the sky, stand here facing towards it. Then look down and you will see your face and eyes. By the way, your eyes are beautiful. Just like all of your face, very nice to see."

Eve: "You are staring again. I must come do this every day with lots of different flowers." "Adam?"

Adam: "Yes."

Eve: "When can we ask God to explain about the circles in the sky? They are so different from each other and they make me wonder."

Adam: "What difference are you thinking about?"

Eve: "There are several. They are the same size, but one is warm and one is not. One is only visible during the daytime and the other is visible at all possible times and keeps changing. One is always a full circle and the other changes shape every day and then starts over again. One you can only look at for a quick glance. The other you can stare at for hours. One is always pale yellow and the other comes in many colors. Why is this?" Adam: "Those are good questions. Next time God visits we'll see what He says. I can name the animals, but I cannot explain the sky."

The next morning Adam finds Eve at the river intently tilting her head this way and that, watching her reflection.

Conclusion

When we remember Eve we should be careful we don't quickly dismiss her as only, the woman who was deceived, fell, and brought calamity to us all. Until her conversation with the serpent, she had never encountered lies, treachery, or deception and was not prepared to expect, suspect, or manage it. We should not be prideful and believe we would not have similarly disobeyed, especially since we disobey God ourselves much too often, and we know better. While it is important for us to keep her mistake in mind, we must not stop there.

We should as well honor her life for the incredible unknown she faced, endured, and overcame. She learned how to be a mother all through trial and error without the help of support groups, how to books, or experiences of other women. Then her discoveries guided countless new mothers that followed.

Eve described the stages of disobedience so we can spot and block them. We will often see temptations, but we can then break the chain by looking away, change our thinking to acceptable topics, or admit our rationalization is bunk.

She left us the wisdom, "Don't even touch it", when we see the presence or approach of temptation. It is a holy principal of endurance for every person of every generation, all over the world. It should be aggressively applied by everyone in pursuit of holiness, which of course should be all of us.

She set the standard very high for lifelong devotion to one husband. Adam lived 930 years and while we are only guessing because the Bible doesn't tell us, Eve was probably with Adam most of that time and she gave him other sons and daughters. They truly did grow old together.

Hannah

Introduction – 1100 BC

Let me introduce you to Hannah, one of the two wives of a man named Elkanah. We are not told where Hannah first lived, whether she was Elkanah's first or second wife, or when, where, or how she died. Her significance to us is found in her loyalty, faith, humility, and motherhood. When we first meet her, she is already married and, painfully childless. She experiences both extremes of motherhood, barren for a while, and then abundantly blessed with children. She deeply understands the hovering pain of the one, and the gushing thrill of the other. She was a lady of honor, an astonishing lady.

Hannah is notable to us for her intense desire to conceive and have a child. She is so dedicated to achieving this joyful experience that she turns to our Lord and makes a vow to return the child to God after she loves on him for a few brief years. I suspect one reason God grants her request is because it is one example of many where women, men, and God Himself, are willing to suffer the loss of a loved one to further the purposes of heaven. God then really blessed her and she not only delivered a son, she delivered Samuel, a prophet, the hands and voice of God in Israel.

Bible account of Hannah in the first and second chapters of First Samuel

Hannah was one of two women married to Elkanah. His other wife, Peninnah, bore him children, but Hannah remained childless. Peninnah taunted Hannah frequently about this. (1:1-7)

Elkanah loved Hannah, provided abundantly for her, and tried to comfort her. (1:5-8)

Elkanah with his wives and children traveled to Shiloh every year for service to God. While there, one year, Hannah stood in the house of the Lord and prayed silently, but with deep conviction. (1:3, 9-13)

Eli, a priest of the Lord, saw her lips moving but heard no sound and accused Hannah of being drunk. She replied that she was not drunk, but instead was praying with the intensity of deep anguish. During the prayer she asked God for a son and made a vow to give her son to the service of God for the rest of his life. (1:13-17)

Eli said to her, "Go in peace, and may the God of Israel grant you what you have asked of him." (1:17)

The conditions were met on both sides. Hannah gave birth to a son and, after he was weaned, Hannah brought him to serve God for the rest of his life. (1:19-27)

Hannah delivers a prayer of praise to honor God. The prayer emphasizes God's sovereignty and provisions. (2:1-10)

Hannah visited her son Samuel every year and brought him a new robe at each visit. (2:19)

God blessed Hannah with more children, sons and daughters. (2:20-21)

Study Questions

1. Hannah knew and tolerated emotional pain and abuse because her husband's other wife could have children, but Hannah could not. While Bigamy is rare now, friction with ex-wives can deliver similar heartaches. If there are children involved, contact with this conflict can last for years. Suggest at least two ways a woman can rise above this distress.

   _____
   _____
   _____

2. Hannah's desire for children was so strong she was willing to make a bargain with God in the form of a two way vow, "If you will do this for me, I will do this in return." Are there situations where we may do that?

   _____
   _____
   _____

3. Hannah suddenly changed from standing and crying out a prayer to going to have a meal. (1 Sa 1:10 & 18) What do think brought about the dramatic change?

   _____
   _____
   _____

4. Hannah released Samuel to the service of the Lord when he was weaned. What age comes to mind when you hear that? What capabilities will Hannah try real hard to equip Samuel with at such a young age?

   _____
   _____
   _____

5. Put your-self in Hannah's position as Samuel's mother and watch him grow as he learns to walk and talk. Might you imagine God slightly delays his growth allowing you a little more time with him?

   _____
   _____
   _____

6. On the trip to deliver Samuel to the care of the Levites, what do you tell Samuel about his purpose? How much courage did they both need for this deeply emotional event? Compare how some children respond to a first day at daycare.

7. Would you expect God with an infinite love for Hannah would bless her with another pregnancy very soon? What considerations weigh on his timing for that?

8. Hannah eventually gave birth to other children and one day they learn about Samuel. Do they silently or vocally wonder if mom will give them away too? How do you comfort a woman today who has to give away her child for some reason?

9. Look at Hannah's prayer in 1 Sa 2:1 – 10. Discuss what you see in verses one and two and then separately, what you see in verses nine and ten.

    Satan Came to Hannah

10. Eventually Hannah will hear about the night her son Samuel heard the voice of the Lord and received a prophecy, (1 Sa 3:2-11). How do you think she will come to accept that? Do you think she bragged about that to her husband's other wife?

Lessons

1. Hannah makes a vow. The Israelites have a mandate from God concerning vows. The requirements for a married woman are found in Numbers 30:10 – 15. According to those verses, any vow Hannah makes remains in force unless her husband nullifies it when he hears about it. Hannah's vow was made silently in a prayer and we don't know when her husband Elkanah learned about it. Whenever Hannah decided to tell Elkanah about her vow, it is very unlikely he would try to nullify it. She remained childless under the efforts he and Hannah made, so why stand in the way of her vow with God? She may have waited until she became pregnant to tell him about the vow and we can imagine her excitement when she told him. We see Elkanah knew about the vow in 1 Sa 1:22 when Hannah said she would take Samuel to live at the temple after he was weaned.
2. We are not to make vows. Today we have a different directive from Jesus. We read it in Matthew 5:33 – 37. When you are ready, read this paragraph in your Bible. Here is a portion of it. Verse 34 says, "But I tell you, do not swear an oath at all…" and verse 37 says, "All you need to say is simply 'Yes' or 'No'; anything beyond this comes from the evil one." This is important to energetically put into practice. It represents a self imposed standard of our highest level of integrity. Our word must be absolute. If we say it, we do it. We do not need to increase the strength of our words by adding a glob of exaggerated promises. Be known for your reliability matching your words. Cute quotes like, "You can take that to the bank," or, "I swear on my mother's grave," tell something about us. They may mean I expect my listener won't believe me so I have to decorate my answer. Actions may speak louder than words but they are a lot slower. So unfortunately, today very few people believe very few other people. Even so, our standard must be a simple yes, or no, and we must stand by it, and we must make it real, every time, every day, for all of our life.
3. Turn the other cheek. Hannah did not retaliate against Peninnah and we are told to behave the same way. Matthew 5:39 says, "Turn the other cheek." Romans 12:17 – 19 says, "Do not repay anyone evil for evil. Be careful to do what is right in the eyes of everyone. If it is possible, as far as it depends on you, live at peace with everyone. Do not take revenge."

Imagine That

1. In the years that followed, we might hear Hannah say, "This week is exceedingly precious to me. We've traveled for four days to Shiloh for our annual temple service and to visit my first born son, Samuel, whom I have given back to God for as long as he lives. I wait all year for this occasion and as the months pass and the day approaches, nearly all of my daydreams are filled with curious hope and imaginings about what I will encounter. I wonder how much has he grown or changed in this last year. Did he miss me, think of me, and pray for me, as I do daily for him? I miss him every hour of every day, but God has blessed me with another son and also, a daughter who will this week, on this annual mission, get to spend time with their older brother."

2. Hannah contemplates. I have again prepared a robe for Samuel; now one of my favorite annual traditions. This robe is different from last year's as, quite happily, I found better yarn and a new color. During our visit each year I stand by Samuel's side and scratch the height of his shoulder on my arm with a thorn. This helps me adjust the size of next year's robe, which I always make a little large so he can grow into it throughout the year. The scratch also leaves a tiny little mark which I treasure while it remains visible. Each reminds me of a moment I was again blessed to be close to my son, Samuel.
3. Hannah is absolutely stunned. She says, "We returned to Shiloh and at the temple we heard the report, God himself has talked with our son Samuel. God called him four times in the night and then gave him a prophecy." This first encounter with God overwhelmed Samuel. Not only did God come and stand near and talk with Samuel, he as well gave Samuel a prophecy. Unfortunately it was not good news for Eli and his sons.
4. Hannah receives blessings in abundance. Hannah rejoices in the rich rewards God has granted her. First, God heard her prayer and gave her Samuel. Second, God honored her fulfillment of her vow and gave her more children, three sons and two daughters. Third, she almost certainly became close friends with Elkanah's other wife, Peninnah. The Bible tells us Elkanah loved Hannah, but it was Peninnah who bore him children. His marriage to each of the women and subsequent treatment of each was obviously different. He gave double portions of meat to Hannah. This may have fostered the animosity demonstrated by Peninnah. She could not make Elkanah favor her, but she could taunt Hannah about a most precious ability of a woman, childbearing. Hannah did not retaliate when she finally had both Elkanah's love and children of her own. She was merciful, and forgiving, and sought to mend the conflict between two competing wives. I am certain this was so because these are the actions of a Godly woman and if you look at her prayer in chapter two, you know she was Godly.

A Short Narrative

The painful day approaches. Hannah reflects, "Every day when I realized I was pregnant, I focused and held on to each moment with this baby inside. My time with Samuel will pass so quickly I must not let the day of our eventual separation enter and torture my heart or mind for even one moment. The day I delivered, with Samuel at last coming to me, though the pain is intense, the process thrilled my soul. I never before experienced something so scary and beautiful at the same time. God held my hand and calmed my breath as I delivered.

As he grows, I delight in sharing these new stages. Samuel stares at birds and cows and smiles when his dad walks in. I am teaching him to walk and it seems like he is sounding out words. I understand the eternal bond between mother and son when I hear his laugh or race to soothe his tears. His tiny hands grip my fingers and his steady breathing warms my neck when he sleeps. Oh, the agony of knowing I must let him go, and the deep reward and peace of knowing I am giving back to God what He gave to me.

A few short years later and now we are just weeks away from our next sojourn to Shiloh. I stare out the window at night and try to imagine about what the future holds for

Samuel. Will he please God? Will he miss me? Of course, of course, yes to both. The love and power that fill him will pour out into God and into me, for life.

I know my time nurturing him is brief and to me, priceless beyond anything else in my life. I help him learn to walk and talk and I share short songs with him to remember. How can I prepare him for what his life will be like? How will I fortify myself with the courage to leave him at the temple? He is nearly weaned now and he sees something new in my eyes which he does not understand. Now, for short moments, I just quietly hold him and say nothing. This year when his dad goes to the temple, he and I will go too. But, now I move slower and hold his hand so much more, and smile at him so often, and hug him tighter than before."

We know Hannah fulfilled her vow and found the strength to let go. We can almost feel how hard it was if we are ever near a daycare center when a child is dropped off for the first time. Within Hannah lives, and we can partially imagine, her mountain of courage.

Every year from then on, when Hannah returned to Shiloh, she would say, "God's love exceeds my understanding and expectations and bursts from Samuel when I hug him." Then God honors her sacrifice with the blessing of additional children to love and nurture.

Conclusion

Hannah trusted the house and priests of God. In 1st Samuel 1:9 we read that in the house of the Lord, after the meal, Hannah stood up. For her it was an act of appeal, a plea for help manifesting itself in a physical attitude of honor to the one appealed to. When a king walks by, you stand. When Hannah called to God, she stood. In church when we ask God to come close, we stand. When Stephen entered heaven, Jesus stood (Acts 7:56). Then after Hannah prayed, scripture says Eli blessed her saying, "Go in peace, and may the God of Israel grant you what you have asked of him (1 Sa 1:17)." Her immediate reaction is in the next verse which says, "Then she went her way and ate something, and her face was no longer downcast." She had faith the words of Eli would come true and her anguish dissipated.

Hannah was merciful. Peninnah tormented her "year after year", but there is no statement that Hannah ever lashed out against her. Hannah ached to fulfill one of God's pleasures for women and she was willing to settle for a short amount of time. Of course, some is better than none. God wove majesty and triumph into the petition in Hannah's prayer. She was willing to give up her son, her only son, just as Abraham was willing to give up his son, his only son, and just as God was willing to give up his only son. At times after giving Samuel back, Hannah wondered how she would go on, but she fortified herself with prayer and faith. Just imagine her courage. Afterward, God blessed Hannah with more children and us with a glimpse of her outstanding life. Hannah, thank you and bless you. I am anxiously waiting for the day I get to meet you.

Lot's Daughters

Introduction – 2070 BC

In the Bible, perhaps a dozen or so towns are the home of stories that imbed themselves into our memories for life. Some of them we learn about for positive and superb reasons such as Bethlehem, Nazareth, Jerusalem, and Capernaum. Then there are towns forever under a dark cloud with a history of shame and drastic endings such as Sodom and Gomorrah. Anyone regularly attending Sunday school has heard about Sodom, the rescue of Lot's family, and the town's final and total fiery destruction. The residents of Sodom routinely participated in so much wickedness that God appeared and told Abraham that He was going to see the town and possibly destroy it. However, we trace two very important women back to Sodom. We first encounter Lot's daughters there, and they become the mothers of the Moabites and Ammonites, two of Israel's strongest, most persistent, antagonists. This chapter is devoted to these two assertive and persistent women.

Their lives were precarious and uncertain in Sodom, but just as their peril is peaking, they escape to a new life. We get to know them under vague identities, as the daughters of Abraham's nephew Lot. The Bible doesn't tell us their names, if they ever marry, or where, when, or how they die. But the Bible does share enough information for us to feel amazed about how they navigate through the events in their lives. Let's start with the direct account from the Bible.

Bible account of Lot's daughters in Genesis chapters 13, 18, & 19

Their father, Lot, was wealthy with livestock and servants. Abraham suggested that he and Lot move to separate vicinities to prevent conflict between their herders. Lot could afford leisure time and was found sitting in the city gate when the two angels arrived. (13:5-7, 19:1)

Knowing that Lot and his family live in Sodom, Abraham negotiates with God asking, "What if only ten righteous people can be found there?" (18:16-33)

Lot's daughters are virgins and pledged to marry men in their town. (19:8, 14)

In order to protect the visitors (angels) in his home, Lot offers his daughters to the men of Sodom to use in whatever way they please. (19:8)

The angels urge Lot to flee the town with his wife and daughters. (19:15)

The four of them leave together, but Lot's wife looks back and becomes a pillar of salt. Lot and his daughters continue on to Zoar and then move on to live in a cave in the mountains. (19:22-30)

The oldest daughter is determined to carry on the family line, tricks her father into participation, and she becomes the mother of Moab. (19:30-33)

The younger daughter repeats the same process with her father the next night and she becomes the mother of Ben-Ammi, the eventual father of the Ammonites. (19:34-38)

Study Questions

1. There are approximately 40 unnamed women in the Bible and Lot's daughters are among them. Why do you suppose the Bible does not tell us their names?
   _____
   _____
   _____

2. In Genesis chapter 13 we develop a strong distaste for Lot when he takes the best land for himself instead of offering it to Abraham. In chapter 19 verses 1-8 Lot offers his daughters to the men of the town to protect the two men in his house. Does our estimation of Lot improve or get much worse?
   _____
   _____
   _____

3. Lot's daughters are virgins and pledged to be married and obedient when told not to look back at the town when they run. How strong is your opinion of their propriety and our concern for their protection and success?
   _____
   _____
   _____

4. Considering the reports about Sodom that God describes to Abraham, (Ge 18:20 – 21), do you wonder why Lot lives there at all and subjects his wife and daughters to a dangerous and depraved community? Do you believe he puts his position and wealth above their safety and well being? Do some men do that today?
   _____
   _____
   _____

5. During the escape from the town of Sodom, Lot's wife looks back and turns into a pillar of salt, (Ge 19:26), and during the fiery destruction, both daughters lose their fiancés. How much courage will their daughters need to continue on over the next few days, while at the same time mourning their losses?
   _____
   _____
   _____

6. For Lot's daughters, how strong is the temptation to go back to Sodom and explore or search for something they can connect with or hold on to? In a parallel, when we have once resisted a temptation, do our defenses relax when the temptation returns and then we give in? How do we keep our position stable and true?

   _____
   _____
   _____

7. Lot's daughters knew a life of privilege and wealth with family and home and then in only a couple days they go to living in a cave. How will this influence their trust, loyalties, and contentment? To what would you go for reassurance and strength if you went from prosperity to poverty and had to start over?

   _____
   _____
   _____

8. The Bible tells us that Lot was seduced by his daughters and they both became pregnant. There are some critics who claim it was Lot who abused his daughters making them pregnant and Bible editors covered that shame to protect Lot. How would you argue for either viewpoint?

   _____
   _____
   _____

9. Follow on question regarding the seduction. What are the chances two daughters would be able to seduce their father on successive nights without him being aware of it and successfully choosing the nights they were both ovulating? Do you see divine intervention at work here, and would that mean God was helping to bring life to Israel's enemies?

   _____
   _____
   _____

10. How do you think Lot's daughters broke the news to him that not only were they both pregnant, but he was the father?

    _____
    _____
    _____

Lessons

1. This account is very well known around the world and serves as a major historical reference for the nation of Israel. Two of their most potent adversaries get their beginning in this story. The lessons Israel learns about steadfastly following, or deciding not to follow God, influenced the trials and triumphs of their nation.
2. When you follow God, sometimes your opponents come from right inside your own family. Consider Isaac verses Ishmael and Jacob verses Esau. In Lot, we find his grandsons become strong opponents to Abraham's grandsons. Portions of Matthew 10:35 & 36 tell us, "a man against his father, a daughter against her mother, and a man's enemies will be the members of his own household."
3. We are rarely able to see the long range plans of God when the situation right in front of us looks very bad. Consider Joseph sold by his brothers to a caravan of Ishmaelites headed to Egypt (Ge 37:12 – 28). Later Joseph rescued the nation of Israel from famine (Genesis chapters 42 – 46). As well, Lot's daughters were mired in a really ugly situation, but their future would improve.
4. God can easily extract something marvelous out of something ugly. Lot's oldest daughter is the mother of the nation of Moab. From that nation, we receive Ruth. She was a Moabite who God placed with Boaz, an Israelite, and together they are listed in the ancestry of David, Solomon, and Jesus (Matthew chapter one).
5. When we join the family of God, leave the old ways behind. Don't look back because there is temptation resting there. Jesus said, "Remember Lot's wife. Whoever tries to save his life will lose it." (Lu 17:32)

Imagine That

1. Lot's daughters remain patient, loyal, and trusting, and agree to flee the town with their father and mother, even after learning two very disturbing realities. First, their father offered them to abuse from the men of the town to protect these two strangers in their home. Second, they suddenly learn that if they escape, they are leaving behind their betrothed husbands. (Genesis 19:16-17) All that and they remain devoted to their family.
2. Lot's daughters, in a flash, under extreme panic, lose their mother, and yet remain strong and smart enough to resist temptation; think about how common it is for a daughter to imitate the actions of her mother. During the escape from Sodom, Lot's wife looked back and became a pillar of salt, but neither daughter followed her actions. They must have a hundred screaming voices in their mind as they run, "Don't look back, Mom where are you, don't look back, don't stop running, Mom, where are you." They must grieve her loss, quickly, silently, internally, while escaping certain death. Imagine the fear, the uncertainty, the extreme terror, and then, imagine their courage. (Ge 19:26)
3. Next, this remarkable event. The oldest daughter will devise and employ a plan to get pregnant and, as a virgin with no personal experience and, with the unlikely ability and participation of an elder and inebriated father, in a cave, she succeeds. She manages to select a time when both she and her sister are ovulating, persuade her father to imbibe, prevent his alarm and refusal regarding her advances, take the

lead in an intimate situation, and convince her sister to take the same steps the next night. Either there is divine intervention at work here, or, she has extreme foresight, situational awareness, instinct, and leadership. (Ge 19:30-38)

A Short Narrative

Lot and his daughters escaped. Three days, and the bulk of the dense black smoke, has passed. The notorious city of Sodom is no more. Soon the winds will erase all remaining evidence of the place where these two sisters were raised. Well known homes, faces, voices, the walk of their mother, and their fiancés all gone in a day. Neither sister witnessed the destruction of their town with their own eyes. If they had, they probably would have died along with their mother.

Their grief cements the bond between them and now it is unshakable. Lot and his daughters fled their town and lost everything; wife and mother, home, friends and connections, livestock and livelihood, and their security, leisure, and peace. Their dismal plight was just beginning to surface the morning after they moved into a cave. None of them knew how cold a cave could be at night. They shivered until their muscles ached. Lot was no longer a young man, ready to rebuild, ready to make a home, and lead the progress of a family. To endure, these two daughters will need energy and insight. Starting today, survival of the family relies on them, and together, they will build their future. It will not be easy. Imagine their courage.

They briefly prioritize their needs. They have sufficient shelter for now; the cave is dreary and cold, but relatively safe. So, they focus on the next essential item, food. When they left their home in Sodom, they grabbed the only thing they could carry in panicked flight, coins. They should have enough money to acquire food nearby in a town, but they need a sustainable source of income. That may be a difficult endeavor. Neither of them is a farmer, merchant, or seamstress.

On the return trip from purchasing food in town, a resource suitable to their situation came into view. A herd of a hundred or more wild goats roam the ravines and crests of the hills near their cave. They could be a source of meat and milk and be traded for other items. How hard can it be to catch a goat? Since neither woman was an experienced trapper, their first attempts will surely come with bruises.

Together they trace the goat's well marked trails and establish a plan. One of them will chase a few goats toward the other and together they will tackle a medium sized prize. It seems plenty simple and easy. However, on the very first try, the goat charges and knocks one of them down, then loses its footing and falls down a cliff, and dies. Well, they won't be trading that one; but, not all is lost. They drag it to the cave and their dad teaches them how to prepare and cook a goat. Lot recommended using a fisherman's net to seize one next time and keep it from harm. They sleep deep that night, but with tough dreams. This new life is rugged.

Capturing with a net took some practice. There were some misses, some cuts and scrapes, and a lot of frustrations. Eventually, they manage to capture a few and mend their wounds. So now, the easy part, we only have to escort them to town for sale. However, unscrupulous characters lurk in surprise places. They were raised in Sodom, a somewhat secure town where harm from rogue vagabonds did not happen. Now they are in outlaw country. The trail to town passes several tight walled ravines with concealed washouts. The women were just setting their pace when three individuals confront them, two in front and one appeared to their rear path. "Give us the goats and leave!"

The women initially cower and back off to the side. With no weapons in sight, suddenly the older daughter is enraged, grabs a large rock and attacks. Screaming and swinging she leaps upon the nearest one. She shouted, "We fought hard to get these and we'll fight hard to keep them". The bandits are taken off guard and she knocks the first one out cold. Her sister joins the fracas swinging and shouting, but the strength of the men overwhelms the women and the other two make off with five of their seven goats. Still shaking, and staring, they shriek at each other, "Can you believe what we just did?" Then they pause, panting, and shaking. They hug their two remaining goats like children. Trembling, they look all around for other danger and then at the unconscious thief. Maternal tendencies take over and they tend his wounds. From then on, they choose to hire escorts from town when they bring a collection of goats in to market.

Eventually they began breeding their own goats because the young offspring are healthier and bring more income. It also results in far less injuries for the sisters. But both of them discover a new feeling that is hard to overcome. Baby goats are cute. They are fun to play with and hard to let go in the market. Dad suggests we keep one or two for pets and the milk is very good. Months pass and their flock increases along with their profits. They are able to provide for their basic needs and some extravagant wants. Better food, blankets, and wine now appear in the cave 'home'. Soon they prepare to obtain a home and leave the damp and cold cave. They are known and respected in town now and when they ask about a home, they find help easily. Everything is going well for the daughters, except for one thing. The women are anxious for family.

The most practical answer would be a husband, but with illnesses and skirmishes, single men are pretty scarce. Every man they meet is either married, or an outlaw, and some of the men they see already have two or three wives. At this rate, what will become of them when their father comes to the end of his life? They need children of their own to assist them in their own old age, as they now do for their father. The women need a new plan and the older daughter gets an idea. "I wonder if we have any more of dad's favorite wine?" she schemes.

Conclusion

If you are appalled at my inclusion of Lot's daughters in this book, please let me explain. I honor each woman in this book for phenomenal courage, and most of them for honorable decisions. The Bible does not scold Lot's daughters for seducing their father or for incest. While it is not a pattern for us to promote, I am not in a position to judge their actions so severely as to leave them out of the book and ignore some valuable lessons. Also, incest was fairly common and tolerated in their culture, but certainly not in ours.

There are a number of things about Lot that are rotten. He would take the best land from Abram, willingly offer his daughters to abuse by an angry mob, and then rear sons born from incest that would become nations of hostility toward all the offspring of his uncle Abraham. Looking back to Genesis chapter 13, we see conflict between Abram and Lot over land and resources. Even so, Abram is very supportive of Lot. He gives Lot first choice on where he will live with his flocks and Abram will take second best. When Lot and his family are captured in Genesis chapter 14, Abram risks his life to rescue Lot, his family, and his possessions. Then, when God visits Abram in person on his way to destroy Sodom and Gomorrah, Genesis chapter 18, Abram stands up to defend the city where Lot lives. "If there are only ten righteous persons there, far be it from you to destroy the righteous with the wicked." (Genesis chapter 18)

A really alarming revelation is waiting on the horizon. One day soon, Lot will suddenly realize his daughters are pregnant, and HE is the father! What! How! When! Have his daughters been discussing how they will explain this to dad when he starts asking questions? Will his first reaction be righteous indignation and anger? Will they break the news to him ahead of time? Will the three of them hide the truth from curious inquirers or throw caution to the wind? Lot's oldest daughter becomes the mother of the Moab nation, and her sister, the mother of the Ammonites. These two nations increase into uncountable descendents and become a continuous bane of Israel for centuries.

While this story is a collection of ugly pieces, I emphasize Lot's daughters because their stern determination and loyalty to family resulted in their permanent place in the origin of two nations. Lot's daughters had fierce willpower to persevere. Each of us should think, "Don't look back," and run on with God no matter what comes our way. We should be accused of having that same intense resolve and family loyalty describe our walk with God.

Mary

Introduction – 20 BC – 40 AD

Who is the most celebrated lady in the history of the world? An angel came to her and said, "Greetings, you who are highly favored. The Lord is with you. You will conceive and give birth to a son and God will give him the throne of David." With enormous faith, this young woman stood face to face with the angel and said, "I am the Lord's servant. May your word to me be fulfilled." Her life will never be the same. She will suddenly be pregnant supernaturally; pretty startling news for a woman of any age, and especially scary for a teenage girl. Friends and family will stare, scoff, whisper, shun, and pray. Angels will come and go and visit your dreams. Wise men will suddenly just drop in with gifts that were perplexing, really, incense and myrrh! She will listen as priests and scholars challenge her son's authority and wisdom, and then cry tears of joy as her son heals countless illnesses. Vast crowds will wait to hear his teachings and then follow him through the towns and across the countryside.

Her name is Mary, most likely the second most well known and popular name of all humanity. She is the mother of Jesus, who is the son of God, the Messiah, the Savior of the world, the creator of all things, and the King on the throne on the right side of God. Mary is the subject of books, the model of sculptors, the inspiration of poets, the vision of painters, the heartbeat of songs, and a child of God.

God tells us the story of Mary in six of the books in the Bible. She has been the subject of countless other books, studies, and movies. She can be approached and learned about from multiple aspects: Holiness, Faith, Devotion, Love, Hope, Heartbreak, and the main focus of this book, Courage. Mary brings us such a powerful presence that we could study her for years and write mountains of pages. I am not worthy to touch her depth. So, for my purpose, to honor her courage, I pull some scripture out of the Bible and then, respectfully and briefly, imagine her courage. Let's get close and know her better.

Bible accounts of Mary from Matthew, Mark, Luke, and John

Moments of magnificent Courage

The situation - Luke 1:26-38. The angel Gabriel visits Mary and tells her these seven truths: 1) You are highly favored, 2) The Lord is with you, 3) The Holy Spirit will come upon you and you will conceive, 4) You will have a son and name him Jesus, 5) God will give Jesus the throne of David, 6) His kingdom will never end, and 7) You aren't alone, one of your relatives, Elizabeth, in her advanced age, is also pregnant and is in her sixth month.

The Moment of Courage - Luke 1:29-30 tells us Mary was greatly troubled and the angel said, "Do not be afraid." Mary overcame her fear and, in verse thirty four, boldly responded to the angel, "How will this be, since I am a virgin?" She is deep in the rush of a thousand thoughts like, "Why am I favored? What is the meaning of this name, Jesus?" and "What do you mean when you say my son's kingdom will never end?" Yet, she challenges the basic notion. She is learning of a plan involving her in a way no other woman in the history of Israel has ever participated in before. She is told her son will be a king, and she says, "Hold on, how can this be? Do you not know? I am a virgin." "Yes of course God knows. That's one of the reasons you are highly favored." Mary is standing there talking with an angel. She thinks "Well maybe you do regularly talk face to face with God, perhaps you can disappear or fly or adjust nature." But, with respect, "Will you please explain this plan to me because I don't understand." Not only is she reverent, willing, enthusiastic, humble, and perplexed, she is also somewhat fearless. Imagine her courage! If I stood face to face with an angel, my tongue and thoughts would freeze up. Mary said, "You can count on me. I am the Lord's."

The situation - Matthew 2:13-14. After the Magi leave, an angel appears to Joseph in a dream and says, "Herod is plotting to kill your son. Flee to Egypt immediately."

The Moment of Courage - Matthew 2:14 says, "So he got up, took the child and his mother during the night and left for Egypt." Let's consider Mary's observations. When she was pregnant and trying to convince Joseph she conceived by the Holy Spirit, he was not easily or fully persuaded. Then in a dream, an angel tells Joseph how she conceived and he accepts the explanation. Now, in the middle of the night Joseph wakes Mary and says, "Our son is in danger. We must leave for Egypt immediately." Here comes the call for Mary to be courageous. Mary must grasp this plan quickly and quell some nagging questions, "What danger? Why now? How will we recognize its approach? Exactly what did the angel say? Did Joseph understand the message clearly? How long will we be gone? Why can't we tell anyone we're leaving or where we are going? Why in the middle of the night?" The Bible doesn't say Mary posed any resistance to the plan, but we can imagine she tried to comprehend the intensity and source of the danger. Why would Herod suddenly want to kill our son? She and Joseph must immediately flee to a foreign country and look over their shoulder the entire time. Imagine the urgency, imagine her courage.

The situation - Luke 2:41-49. This is the account of Mary and Joseph traveling, when Jesus is twelve years old, to Jerusalem for the Festival of the Passover. When the family starts the journey back home to Nazareth, Jesus remains behind in Jerusalem. Believing Jesus is in the caravan, his parents travel on for a day. When they discover their son is absent, they search among their fellow travelers with no success. Then they return to Jerusalem and continue the search.

Moment of Courage – Luke 2:45-46 tells us, "When they did not find him, they went back to Jerusalem to look for him." Now insert yourself into Mary's shoes. When a child vanishes, a mother could both panic like a horse spotting a rattlesnake, and at the same time, turn over every stone for a thousand miles searching for her child. She would not rest, sleep, eat, slow down, or give up. She would stand up to any adversary to defend her child. Mary bravely faced the unknown with severe determination. Just try to imagine her courage. After three days they found him in the temple. Then, just when she should be able to relax and get some sleep, she is further confounded when Jesus says, "Didn't you know I had to be in my father's house"?

<u>The situation</u> – Matthew 27:55, Mark 15:40, and John 19:25. These three Bible sections tell us Mary, the mother of Jesus, was present and watching the crucifixion. She can't leave, or stay, or understand.

<u>The Moment of Courage</u> – There are mixed reactions among humans who observe the agony of another human. Some won't look at all. Some will briefly look to be able to understand and confirm the truth. Some will watch for awhile to gain the closure of knowing this issue is done. However, for the people who are attached one way or another to the person in agony, the process is completely different. While they are skipping back and forth through the five stages of grief; denial, anger, bargaining, depression, and acceptance, they are also clinging to hope and searching for solutions they can apply to change the situation. All these were pushing and tugging at Mary's heart.

She stood at the cross confused, devoted, afraid, anxious, and hopeful. This is her son who needs her help and this is the king who should not be treated this way. She doesn't know how to fix this wrong, and she can't ignore it. She stands and waits and prays and hopes and aches to run to him and, at the same time, to run away. Comments from others there adjust her hopes or fears. Some yell taunts of disgrace while others voice feelings of reverence. A thousand times she silently asks herself, "What do we do now, what do I do now?" If stress paralysis was understood, she might be very familiar with it now. Stand there with her now and for a few minutes, imagine her courage.

Then Jesus speaks directly to her and releases her from her feelings of denial and anger. Referring to John, Jesus says to her, "Woman, here is your son." (Jo 19:26)

Study Questions

1. We first meet Mary in Luke 1:27 where the angel Gabriel surprises her with, "Greetings, you who are highly favored." At that point in time with no report on her early life, speculate on why she was "highly favored".

2. Gabriel told Mary she would conceive and give birth to a son. Why do you think Mary asked "How can this be, since I am a virgin?" instead of just assuming the angel referred to a pregnancy that would occur after she was married to Joseph?

3. Mary goes to visit Elizabeth who suddenly shouts to her, "Blessed are you among women." (Lu 1:42) In what way would Mary agree with that assessment?

4. When Joseph learns Mary is pregnant, certainly he must ask for an explanation, but he doesn't accept her answer, or he would not consider a quiet divorce. Not only does he not believe her, he is instead considering any other explanations, which means he believes she is deceiving him or unstable. If he doesn't believe her now, how confident is she in their future together?

5. Read Luke 2:28 – 35. Gabriel said her son would have the throne of David. Now Simeon says her son will be spoken against and a sword will pierce her soul too. How does Mary balance these two extremes in her repeating daydreams?

6. Three men knock on the door and ask, "Where is the king of the Jews. We have come to worship him?" (Mt 2:2) How much does this astound Mary? Then, their gifts add to the confusion. It's not blankets or bread. It is incense, myrrh, and gold. How well can she assign meaning to those three gifts?

_____
_____
_____

7. Suddenly Joseph wakes Mary, "We have to take Jesus immediately to Egypt. We can't tell anyone we are leaving or where we are going." Now Mary must find exceptional internal courage. In her heart race the questions, "Where is the danger? How long will we be gone? Why does Joseph believe this now?" How does Mary cope with this unexpected and drastic change to her simple, routine life as a mom?

_____
_____
_____

8. Now, leap forward to when Jesus is twelve years old and missing. Mary and Joseph search and find him in the temple reasoning with the teachers of the law. Do you think Mary still feels up to the task of raising the son of God?

_____
_____
_____

9. As a mom, or aunt, or sister, as a parallel to Mary, express the joy you feel when you notice God at work in the life of someone you love, as Mary must have felt when she asked Jesus to provide wine for the wedding, (John 2:1-5).

_____
_____
_____

10. Now, leap forward again. Mary's first child has been unfairly persecuted and hangs on a cross with his death imminent and certain. Your heart screams for relief for him and yourself. How can the God who miraculously impregnated you abandon His son and you now? What would you tell her?

_____
_____
_____

Lessons

1. In the book of John 2:3-11, we read. This is the first written miracle, the wedding banquet when Jesus turned the water into wine. The situation is well recorded and often discussed by Bible readers today. The focus is on the resistance of Jesus, the volume of water involved, and the quality report by the master of the banquet, "You have saved the best wine for last." It was probably the purest and best wine ever on earth. Notice the steps; put water in, take wine out. Jesus usually requires people to take action to activate miracles; they are powered by faith. This is great joy for us to think about. But, don't quit there. Tucked in the dialogue between mother and son are five words of outstanding guidance for us. When Jesus responds, "Why do you involve me? My hour has not yet come", notice Mary's response. It is eternal guidance in five words. She said to the servants, "Do whatever he tells you." This should be a self imposed mandate for us. Whenever we come to Jesus, when something needs repair, when relationships are sour, when turmoil follows us; then we should apply her words and "Do whatever he tells you." There are several ways He can tell you what He wants you to do; in your prayers, in a friend's prayer, in a pastor's sermon, in a Bible reading, or in the kind words of an acquaintance. So, when he speaks to you, remember Mary's advice and "Do whatever he tells you." That guideline is good for life. Always apply it.
2. When God visits you in a dream, trust it. An angel visited Joseph three times in his dreams and the message in each involved Mary. The first dream was positive for both of them and confirmed two things. First, Joseph was close to and listening to God, and second, Mary's child was indeed conceived by the Holy Spirit. The second dream might have met with a little skepticism in Mary, but she promptly responded in full support as they left for Egypt. Once she accepted the dream, then the fear of the danger was offset by her trust in God's protection. In Egypt, Mary waited and hoped for a third dream and, when Joseph received it, Mary enthusiastically embraced it. Now they could go home.

Imagine That

God said to Mary, "I am sending you messengers who will speak words from heaven to you, some too wonderful for you to understand. As you lay awake at night and pray, remember their words and watch them unfold." Store these up in your heart:

The angel Gabriel visited Mary and said, "You will conceive and give birth to a son, and you are to call him Jesus. He will be great and will be called the Son of the Most High. The lord God will give Him the throne of his father David, and he will reign over Jacob's descendants forever; his kingdom will never end." (Luke 1:31 – 33) This is a pretty large message for a young teenage girl.

Shepherds visit the stable and share the angel's message, "I bring you good news that will cause great joy for all the people. Today in the town of David a Savior has been born to you; he is the Messiah, The Lord. This will be a sign to you. You will find a baby wrapped in cloths and lying in a manger." (Luke 2:10-12, 19) In verse 7, she had just wrapped him in cloths and placed him in a manger. The shepherds are reporting to her how they saw the sky full of angels singing and her son is the long awaited Messiah.

Mary thinks, "I heard a similar prophecy nine months ago. I wonder why God is bringing the Messiah into the world in a barn."

Mary and Joseph take Jesus to the temple on the eighth day and Simeon meets them and says, "This child is destined to cause the falling and rising of many in Israel and to be a sign that will be spoken against" (Luke 2:34). Mary thinks, "We have heard about this in a barn and now again in the temple. That confirms the shepherd's message."

There is a knock at the door and three well dressed men enter. They bow down and worship her son who is close to the age of two. Then they give her gifts of gold, frankincense, and myrrh (Mt 2:11). This surprise is unexpected, what can it mean? Three men with gifts are worshipping our son. I knew he was special but I am still overwhelmed.

Consider the four topics above. Mary was gradually recognizing their reality in her life. The magnitude of her responsibility becomes clearer every day. She takes a deep breath, stands tall, and proceeds. Imagine her courage.

Shortly after the Magi leave, an angel visits the dream of Joseph and tells him to take Mary and Jesus and leave for Egypt (Matthew 2:13 – 14). Mary thinks, "Now I get it. The Magi showed up with gold a few days ago because we would need means of support for our trip to Egypt." I wondered about such an extravagant gift. However, I'm still wondering about the incense and myrrh.

Traveling merchants passing through the square in Egypt report vague accounts of a murderous rampage in Bethlehem a year ago. There is terrible anguish and depression there for every family that lost a son under the age of two. No one in Bethlehem can explain it. With the Magi gone, no one knew why Herod sent soldiers to kill young boys. Mary notes we escaped just before that. Could that slaughter have been because of us? Mary and Joseph feel certain the danger remains and they must not tell anyone about the timing and reason they left Bethlehem.

A Short Narrative

In Egypt Mary sits staring, speechless, hands fidgeting. She ponders a wide variety of thoughts. I can see the pyramids on the horizon, thirty miles to the west. After a year here, I still suffer from culture shock. The ceremonies we regularly participate in to connect with God are buried behind pagan ritual here. Joseph and I are very careful to avoid the places of worship the locals frequent. We also stay close to home on days of mandatory ceremonies to their gods. The chanting, and music, and revelry seem to call people to come and celebrate. It is not for us. God has warned Israel for centuries to avoid the gods of our neighboring nations.

I miss my mom and dad, and the friends I grew up with. Our future seems so uncertain, we pray but can't discover a tangible feel for what to expect. This is not our home, we hope. There is a language here that I don't want Jesus to learn, but he seems to learn so fast and, while it is impressive, it is also frightening.

Jesus seems so mature for his age. He is only three and yet he imitates us like an adult. I found him on knees praying the way we do. Eyes closed, hands folded, for half an hour. Then he opened his eyes, smiled, and went out to play. Also, a week ago, I heard James, our second son, cry in the night, and when I went to see him, Jesus was already there soothing his woes like a parent would.

Something puzzles me. Several times in the last six months I was sure I was almost out of flour and oil, but when I checked again the containers were full. Then, when all of our neighbors were hit hard by locusts, we were not. I know God blesses those who follow him, but this seems personal, concentrated right in our home. There are some local kids who tease and bully the younger ones in the area, but they are constantly respectful toward Jesus. I marvel at it all, but say nothing.

Most alarming of late was a day we were out for a hike on the plains. I sat down to rest and Jesus walked out a couple hundred feet, but still in my view. Suddenly a dozen or so camels came in a charge over a hill and bolted straight at Jesus. On my feet in a flash, I ran shouting but the camels were much faster. My heart raced and screamed and so did I. In seconds the camels would be upon Jesus and I shrieked in panic. Then, I declare, every camel stopped just feet from him and kneeled down. He didn't flinch. Then casually, like he knew them, he walked over and patted the head of each one. They rubbed against him and he laughed, and then I joined in, all my fears released.

Perhaps Jesus has some connection with nature that I don't understand. On the hottest of days, Jesus will stand at the window, bow his head, and minutes later a nice cool breeze arrives very quietly and gently. He never seems frustrated by, or afraid of, anything, and he is always at peace with every situation.

Update on Joseph. When I first met him he was pretty faithful to the Lord. He met all the duties of a devoted man of God. But now, after the angel advised him in a dream about fleeing the danger in Bethlehem, and then hearing reports of how it came true, Joseph is on fire. Here in Egypt there are small groups of us who attach ourselves to the God of Moses and Abraham, and we are surrounded by communities who worship lots of other gods. Even so, Joseph eagerly explores the scrolls of Isaiah and inquires of priests, and prays like a priest himself. He is very open about his faith, even though there are so few of us here. He and I agreed to keep silent about the warning of the angel and our quick escape from home because we feared the danger would follow us here.

The angel who first came to me said our son Jesus would receive the throne of David, so we know eventually we will return to our homeland. We just don't know when this may happen and so we are making the best progress we can here.

Joseph shows me every day how much he loves me. I catch him staring at me with a smile on his face. He helps with care for our boys and chores at home after he is done with woodwork for the day.

I am blessed beyond what my most rational imagination could expect. Joseph had a new visit in his dream last night and my heart skips with joy. We are going home!

Conclusion

Mary is the only person to witness, see, hear, and cry over all three of the most fantastic events in all the history of all humanity: 1) The birth of Jesus, the Son of God, 2) The death of Jesus, the Lamb of God, and 3) The resurrection of Jesus, the King of Kings and Lord of Lords. She saw the power, tragedy, and majesty; and after each she could still breathe, but just barely. Every possible emotion she could ever feel found expression in at least one of these three events. After the first event she slept, after the second she mourned, and after the third, she danced.

Then Mary treasured all these things up in her heart and pondered them. (Lu 2:19)

Naomi

Introduction – 1280 – 1320 BC

The Bible is like a time machine; open it to any page and climb in. It faithfully takes us to dramatic events, historic times, people, and places so important that God himself ensured they were recorded for everyone in all future generations. He planted the knowledge in the authors, motivated them to write the account, and then guarded the Bible for our guidance, understanding, and benefit. One of the people God wants us to meet is Naomi, the wife of Elimelek and the mentor of Ruth. Ironically her whole story is found in the book of Ruth, named after the daughter-in-law she tried to leave behind in Moab. We can vividly see and hear through the eyes and ears of Naomi as we explore the book of Ruth in the Bible.

Naomi lived during the centuries when Israel was led by appointed judges and national faith in God wavered like the weather. During this period, according to Judges 17:6, "Israel had no king and everyone did as they saw fit." Even though her story occurs during a time of calm between Israel and Moab, everyone knows the history of conflict both sides generated, and it still overshadowed any connections across the border.

Naomi's life was a tale of two extremes. She enjoys the days of plenty, and referred to her days as full with family. Then misfortune comes her way and she loses the plenty and the family. Yet, she holds God in high esteem and her loyalty impresses a young woman to do the same. With her husband and two sons, Naomi moves from Bethlehem to Moab and her sons may marry Moabite women. So, what does that mean to Naomi and her family?

First, God imposed restrictions on Moabites, forbidding them and their descendants down to ten generations, from entering the assembly of the Lord. Second, God prohibited treaties of friendship with Moab for life (Deuteronomy 23:3 – 6).

Naomi knows her sons will be tempted to marry Moabite women and if they do, their wives and children will not be allowed in the house of the Lord when they return to Israel. The potential for family disruption will follow Naomi around for many years. However, Naomi and God work together and work Ruth into the line of David, Solomon, and Jesus. Let's go see how she fares.

Bible account of Naomi in the book of Ruth

Naomi was blessed with a husband named Elimelek and two sons named Mahlon and Kilion. They were from Bethlehem, but there was a famine in the land, so they went to live in Moab. (1:1-2)

While they lived in Moab, Elimelek died and his sons married Moabite women named Orpah and Ruth. Then, both of Naomi's sons died also. (1:3-5)

Naomi heard reports that the Lord was blessing Bethlehem with good crops again, so she prepared to return to her homeland. Part of the preparation included persuading Orpah and Ruth to return to the homes of their parents in Moab. Orpah agreed and left, but Ruth determined to go anywhere Naomi went and proclaimed an oath of lifetime allegiance. (1:6-18)

Naomi and Ruth arrive in Bethlehem during the 'barley harvest' time of year. Their arrival surprises the people who knew Naomi from way back when she lived there before. (1:19-22)

Ruth goes out in search of food and work. She enters a field belonging to Boaz and impresses him and his workers with her diligence and integrity. (2:1-7)

Boaz and Ruth discuss the fields, her freedom to work there and her safety. Boaz compliments her loyalty to Naomi, her mother-in-law. (2:8-12)

Boaz arranges for Ruth to have enough food and take some home to Naomi. (2:13-16)

Ruth and Naomi discuss the work, the fields, Ruth's safety, and of course, Boaz, a relative of Naomi's, through her late husband. (2:17-22)

Naomi suggests a plan to test and attract Boaz to care for Ruth. The plan requires great daring on the part of Ruth. She is to slip in quietly in to the threshing barn in the dark of night and lay down at the feet of Boaz as he sleeps. Imagine her courage. She is totally successful and when Boaz wakes he asks, "Who are you?" When he learns it is Ruth and he is her redeemer, he is very pleased. (3:1-9)

Boaz tells Ruth there is one redeemer closer than himself and they must allow him to have first choice to redeem or not. Then Boaz sends her home with more food. (3:10-17)

Naomi tells Ruth the matter will be settled today. (3:18)

Boaz convenes a meeting of elders and the other kinsman-redeemer. Boaz bundles the property of Naomi to include the possession of Ruth. This spooks the redeemer and he declines the right and turns it over to Boaz. (4:1-8)

Boaz redeems Ruth, marries her, and together they have a son. (4:9-13)

Naomi's friends praise her status and blessings coming from God through Ruth and Boaz, and their son Obed. (4:14-17)

Study Questions

1. Naomi is familiar with stress. There is a major famine in her region of Israel and God is silent. Her family is considering a move to a foreign nation. Will this cause her, and would this cause you, sleepless nights?

   _____
   _____
   _____

2. Settling in to a new land and leaving behind well known surroundings and friends brings challenges. What may Naomi turn to for reassurance and comfort now?

   _____
   _____
   _____

3. Read Ruth 1:3 – 5 and watch the focus of Naomi's affection shift from her husband to her sons, and then to their wives. A lot of women outlive their husbands and we witness their transitions to new lives. How is it easier, if it ever is, for a woman who has many years of contact with God, as Naomi did?

   _____
   _____
   _____

4. How do we know Naomi still displayed a loyalty to God after her sons died? See Ru 1:8-9 & 2:20.

   _____
   _____
   _____

5. Read Ruth 1:11 – 13 where Naomi explains why both of her daughter-in-laws should return to their own families. Do you think Naomi presented a reasonable argument? What situation might Naomi have failed to consider that would prevent either woman from returning to her own home?

   _____
   _____
   _____

6. Naomi returns to Bethlehem with Ruth and surprises the towns citizen's who remember her. Read Ruth 1:19 – 21 and compare question four with Naomi's response to their greeting.

   _____
   _____
   _____

7. In Ruth 1:20, Naomi tells the towns folk, "Don't call me Naomi, call me Mara because the Lord has made my life very bitter." Then she adds that she went away full but has returned empty. How is Naomi measuring her wealth?

   _____
   _____
   _____

8. Ruth goes to work in a field belonging to Boaz and Naomi identifies him as a guardian redeemer (Ruth 2:20). Read Deuteronomy 25:5 – 10 about redeemer responsibilities and explain how that fits Ruth's situation.

   _____
   _____
   _____

9. Read Ruth 3:2-4 where you will see the plan Naomi prepared for Ruth. She tells Ruth to look her best and then go approach Boaz in a quiet humble fashion. Do you think Naomi is using a mild form of deception or glamour advertising to compel Boaz into desiring Ruth?

   _____
   _____
   _____

10. Examine the verses in Ruth 4:14 – 16 and explain the two part happy ending. In 4:17, why do the women say, "Naomi has a son!" Consider Deuteronomy 25:6. Would that verse apply?

    _____
    _____
    _____

Lessons

1. Naomi has a remarkable sense of where true value is in life. For her, it is not possessions or monetary wealth, but family. She says she left Bethlehem full, with a husband and two sons, but returned empty, without all three (Ru 1:21). She did not define full or empty as a measure of money. It is a lesson for us to remember the high value of family and friends, and work to never take them for granted.
2. Naomi's faith in God was strong. We read her report that God's hand was against her, (Ru 1:13) and her declaration, "Call me Mara (which means bitter) because the almighty has made my life very bitter" (Ru 1:20). From those two statements we could easily think she turned away from God. But consider this. There are dozens of accounts in the Bible where the Israelites settled into a community where the local residents worshiped other gods. Then pretty quickly, they adopted and worshiped the local gods as their own. We do not see this with Naomi. The Moabites worshiped Chemosh and later, Solomon, the king of Israel, did the same (1 Ki 11:7). The Bible records no action by, or against, Naomi involving the worship of false gods. However sour Naomi was about God, she still held Him up with such reverence that Ruth was determined to make Him hers. Remember Ruth saying, "Your God will be my God"? (Ru 1:16). God was attractive in the life of Naomi. When life throws trials at us, are we still so obviously loyal to God that other people will be drawn to Him? We should consider the trials as temporary challenges and lessons, but devotion and attachment to God are eternal.

Imagine That

1. Do any of Naomi's actions fit the title of this book? Where in her story do we witness and admire her courage? There are at least three events that reveal this quality in her. First, consider her willingness to move to a foreign land, and to move back. Second, she took on the duty of mentoring Ruth. Last, she trusted God's control over her life. All these are segments of her life requiring great courage and she faces each head on. But there is also a painful series of events that require her steadfast courage. They are the deaths of three very close family members; her husband and both sons. That this deeply affects her surfaces when she tells the town's people, "Call me Mara because I am bitter." This is her only documented response, but there is much more. There are five stages of grief and the stage of "Denial" requires enormous courage to transition out of and into the stage of "Acceptance." Many people facing a loss will for weeks or months say, "It's not real, I don't want to think about it now" and "I don't want to force myself to accept it just yet, I can't face it now," or "I can't let go yet". Eventually, they will stand up and say, "Okay, I am ready to admit I have to go on without them." It is very painful and takes a lot of courage. Naomi was hit with this three times in ten years; she lost her husband and outlived both of her sons. Just try to imagine her courage. She clearly fits the goal of this book, to honor her courage.
2. Naomi's delight in God changed. The name Naomi means "pleasant". When she meets the residents of her hometown, she says, "Call me Mara because God has made my life bitter." (Ruth 1:20 – 21) Mara means "bitter". The author of the book

of Ruth continues to call her Naomi throughout the entire book and notice the name the town's people use for her when she becomes a grandmother. In Ruth 4:17, they say, "Naomi has a son". They are again, or still, calling her Naomi (pleasant).
3. Naomi mentors Ruth. She understands Boaz is focusing on business at the time of harvest. He may be kind to Ruth with protection and food (Ruth 2:8 & 9), but fail to consider her potential as a promising mate. Maybe Boaz needs a little nudge or encouragement. Naomi prepares Ruth, making her as appealing as possible, to catch his eye. "Wash, perfume yourself, and put on your best clothes" (Ruth 3:3). But then instructs her to approach Boaz in the most humble way she can imagine. "Watch where he lays, go and uncover his feet and lie down" (Ruth 3:4). Naomi's plan meets with success; Boaz is honored and takes action to take her as a wife. Happy ending for everyone because Ruth gives birth to a son and the town attaches the importance of the event into Naomi's family line.

A Short Narrative

The Journal and Journey of Naomi

Though always in God's loving hands, sometimes I cannot see
When trials and fears come along, you walk right next to me.
We fought a famine in our land, but gave up in despair.
Then looking back, I see it now, we were in your care.
So soon in the new land, my husband passed away.
Why were you quiet then, as I prayed and cried all day.
I finally forgave you on the days my sons were wed
Then you forgave me too, and raised my soul and head
We never can be sure, about what fills our lives
So I hold to this delight, both my sons have wives.
In these days, I brag of you, the God who loves me so
And I hoped this joy would last, but little could I know
The sons I bore are no more, and so I hurt inside
Let everyone know, it is so, this pain I will not hide.

Intermission – We wait while Naomi and Ruth travel to Bethlehem
And now, part two

A new purpose comes to me, guide this woman Ruth
Who gives her all to me, her life, her faith, her truth.
My hometown welcomes us, and oh the questions fly
No husband or sons, let us mourn, when did they die?
Ladies shush, see here how, I am blessed with Ruth
She gives me her love, her strength, and her youth
Let us work together for this woman needs a plan
Share your thoughts and then, help her find a man
Meanwhile, in the fields, God and Ruth proceed

> To match her up with Boaz, a Godly man indeed
> When they wed, Naomi smiles, and God says it is good
> Before too long, Ruth will know, the joy of motherhood
> Ruth will rear a son who'll soothe our tears and pain
> Let everyone know, it is so, this joy I can't contain

Conclusion

God was right there in Naomi's life, leading, making changes, planting ideas, and adjusting circumstances. He encouraged and strengthened her and worked through her to employ his plans. She lost some family members and gained others. She couldn't see it, but her efforts to help Ruth resulted in her own connection to the ancestry of King David and the whole line down to Jesus.

At times Naomi was bitter and said God's hand was against her. That certainly sounds like us at times, and we do it for much smaller reasons than family deaths. How easy is it for us to blame God when we don't get a raise at work, a close seat at entertainment, the house, car, or spouse of our choice, or when there is a dark spot on an X-ray. Even with the loss of three loved family members, Naomi still made God so special that Ruth said, "I am going with you and your God will be my God"

How can we be sure we hold God up high even during adversity? Practice the habit during the calm pleasant times and it will come more naturally during trials. Review the reasons you believe God loves you and keep them firmly in your thoughts. Then, adopt a prayer used by Jesus, "Not my will, but thine" (Matthew 26:39).

Rahab

Introduction – 1395 BC

Rahab was a resident of Jericho and a great strategist. She had a vision for the future and could interpret the signs of current events. She knew the best choice for the way ahead was to join up with the Lord and His plans. That same choice is true for us. Rahab lived in Jericho and Joshua was headed her way to take the city. Joshua sent two spies into the city for reconnaissance; Rahab intercepted them. As they talked she told them how the people in Jericho knew God was giving the Israelites victory in battle and the whole town of Jericho was in fear. She hid the spies on her roof under stalks of flax when the town officials came looking for them. For her assistance in protecting them, she was promised that she and her family would be spared in the coming attack if she placed a scarlet cord in her window. It would be a signal to every Israeli soldier approaching the walls of Jericho.

All Rahab had to do was bring her family to her home just before the Israelites attacked. How hard could that be?

Bible account of Rahab in the book of Joshua chapters two and six

Joshua sent two spies to look over the town of Jericho. They stayed with Rahab, a prostitute. (2:1)

The King of Jericho sent Rahab a message to bring the spies out. She told the messengers that the men had already left and they should leave at once to catch up to them. Truth was she hid them on her roof under stalks of flax. (2:2-6)

Rahab told the spies that everyone in Jericho was afraid of the Israelites because God had helped them defeat their enemies and had dried up a river so they could cross over on dry land.(2:8-11)

Rahab made an agreement with the spies, their lives for hers. The spies told her to place a scarlet cord in her window and she and her family would be spared during the attack. (2:12-14, 17-18)

Jericho was securely barred because the Israelites were near. No one entered or left the city. (6:1)

The Israelites marched around Jericho once a day for six days. Each time they carried the Ark of the Covenant of the Lord and seven priests blew trumpets. (6:3-4)

For six days the Israelites got up each morning, lined up the priests and soldiers, and marched around the city. Then they returned to their camps for the night. (6:11-14)

On the seventh day, the Israelites marched around the city seven times. Then Joshua gave all the soldiers the command to shout. (6:15-16)

As the soldiers shouted, the walls of Jericho collapsed and the soldiers ran straight in. (6:20)

Joshua told the two spies to rescue Rahab and all the family with her in her home in agreement with their oath. (6:22-23)

Biblical account of Rahab in Matthew, Hebrews, and James

Rahab went on to become the mother of Boaz who married Ruth. So Rahab was the great-great-grandmother of King David. (Matthew 1:5)

Because of her abundant faith, Rahab was spared when Jericho fell. (Hebrews 11:31)

Rahab, a prostitute, was considered righteous because she hid the spies. (James 2:25)

Study Questions

1. Consider the account of Rahab in Joshua chapter two. She hid the Israeli spies on her roof under stalks of flax. Then she told the king's messengers who were searching for them that the men had left before the city gate was closed. Would we think of her as strategically wise or ruthlessly deceptive?

   _____
   _____
   _____

2. Now, notice in verses 8 – 14 the strength of several give and take conditions. Rahab argues in favor of the Israelites, "I know the Lord has given you this land. So, I want to join you." The spies know they are indebted to her for their lives, on one hand, but also trapped on her roof and vulnerable to her raising the alarm about their presence. Same question as before. Would we think of Rahab as wise or ruthless?

   _____
   _____
   _____

3. In verses 2:9 – 11, how is Rahab encouraging the Israelite spies to take back a report that motivates their army to take the city?

   _____
   _____

4. In the same verses, 9 – 11, can you identify how Rahab respects and fears the God of Israel, but probably does not claim him as her Lord as yet?

   _____
   _____

5. Review chapter two verses 12 – 13 and weigh the volume of people in Rahab's rather large request. It could easily add up to a dozen or more people Rahab is asking to save. Do you think the fact that she has the spies in a risky position emboldens her to ask for so much? Why do you suppose she doesn't ask for the lives of friends?

   _____
   _____
   _____

6. Rahab lives in an apartment with a window in the city wall. Do you think that might be convenient, dangerous, or both?

_____

_____

_____

7. Is there anyway Rahab could have known the Israelites would not attack the first time they marched around the city?

_____

_____

_____

8. On the fourth, fifth, and sixth days of the marching Israeli soldiers, take the place of Rahab and describe how you would persuade your family back to your home.

_____

_____

_____

9. How well do you expect a prostitute blended into the Israeli world when Rahab joined them? Consider Matthew 1:5.

_____

_____

_____

10. After the battle of Jericho, how do you think God feels about Rahab? Consider James 2:25.

_____

_____

_____

Lessons

1. Rahab tells the two spies from Israel three details of importance. First, I know the Lord has given you this land. Second, the people in this town heard how the Lord dried up the Red Sea when you came out of Egypt, and they all live in fear of you. Third, we also heard how the Lord helped you defeat the kings of Sihon and Og. Then Rahab asks to join the Israelites and offers to help them. (Joshua 2:8-11) Rahab declared that she wanted to join the family of God and she described why. She saw what life with the Lord looks like; she saw that life is promising and victorious. She was willing to leave her failed life with false gods and idol worship behind. That is a lesson for us because it is the exact same process we go through. First we see the love and peace present in the family of God and we compare our frustrating, meaningless pursuits. The overwhelming contrast generates our desire to be a member of God's family.
2. Rahab could not see how the Lord's plan would unfold, but she kept faith that He was in control. On the first day the Israelites marched around the city, she thought, "Here we go, this is it." Then, the same marching and expectations occur on the second, third, and fourth days. No one could tell her about the plan, so she just needed to trust in God, and wait. It is sometimes the same for us. We may not understand the direction God is leading us in, the people involved, the delay for action, or the sacrifices we are asked to make, but we must always trust that the outcome is well known and prepared by God. It might be confusing or pretty scary along the way. So, stay constant in prayer and let God run the show. You are going to love how the story ends. Rahab did not know the plan of the Lord, but she was ready when the time came.

Imagine That

1. Stopping at the residence of a prostitute was a reasonable cover plan for the two spies. It was not unusual for travelers to pay her a visit. The spies knew this would appear to be their intention and that would reduce the local citizen's scrutiny of them. Rahab realized they were spies before the king's messengers told her so. This is evident because she hid them on her roof under stalks of flax.
2. Prostitutes were tolerated, but not respected. It was a difficult way of life for Rahab. Most people in town kept their distance from her. That may have contributed to her so quickly making an alliance with the spies instead of turning them in to protect the town. Rahab may have already been leaving the life of a prostitute when the spies arrived and she joined their culture. The stalks of flax on the roof could indicate she was transitioning into a new income.
3. The treaty and plan with the spies seemed simple enough to Rahab; the Israelites arrive, attack, and her family is spared. But, anxiety probably set in at the start. When to place the cord in the window? Would it be visible enough to work? Was there a risk it would draw the attention of soldiers guarding the city? Tie the cord in, take the cord out, open the window, close the window, block it part way. Whew! Pace all day, fret all night, adrenaline up, appetite down. Is this ever going to work out?

4. Rahab had a long list of family members she wanted protected; father, mother, sisters, brothers, and all who belong to them. Notice there is no mention of friends; perhaps very few people have close relationships with prostitutes.
5. Rahab is strategically wise and instructs the spies on how to avoid capture. She lives in a house that is part of the city wall and lowers the men to the ground from the window. Very convenient for anyone wishing to leave unseen; possibly a covert method she was used to employing.

A Short Narrative

A play titled - Any Day Now
Cast of Characters
Rahab
Two Israeli Spies
Beth - Rahab's mother
Amos - Rahab's Father
Leah - Rahab's Sister
Ben - Rahab's Brother, a soldier in Jericho
Setting – The Town of Jericho, a walled town ten miles north northwest of the Dead Sea.
Date – Approximately 1402 BC.

Scene One – In the market square, Rahab is strolling and pretending to shop. Actually, she is looking for the two foreigners she saw approaching town from her window. She immediately knew who they were, and when they entered the city gate she knew she must talk to them. She finds them at a leather works counter and nudges one of them. Imagine her courage.

Rahab: Might I have a word in private, my lord? It is urgent and very important.
Spy: (Hesitant) Are you referring to me? I do not know you!
Rahab: (Quietly) Please, listen carefully. I know who you are and why you are here, but you are in serious danger and must trust me. I will help you, but we cannot talk here. We are being watched, so do what I say. Look only at me, lean in close and whisper something. Then let people see you hand me some money. I'll nod and point away, and then you two follow me to my apartment. Surely you are not afraid of one woman. Remember, I know who you are, but I have not raised an alarm.

Scene Two – At Rahab's apartment, behind closed doors, the three can now talk quietly. Rahab returns their money and offers water and fruit to gain their trust.

Spy: (Anxious) Okay, talk. How do you know us and what is this danger you speak of?
Rahab: The whole town knows who you are and suspects why you are here. You are advance spies for Israel, and if you are in Jericho we are your next target. We anticipated and feared your arrival. The authorities are even now deciding what to do with you. The citizens of Jericho have heard the reports of your victories and goals. Now that you have

seen the inside of our walls you are a risk they cannot allow. They will come to stop you from leaving. We must move fast and conceal you.

Spy: (Abruptly to other spy) I think we should just leave now, and quickly.

Rahab: You cannot go now; the guards at the gates will be told to watch for you. Follow me to the roof, I have a plan. When you return, remember I could have turned you in, but spared you.

Spy: By our word, when we come to conquer Jericho, you and anyone in this apartment with you will be spared. So our soldiers can identify your location, mark your window with this scarlet cord. It will be a signal to us.

Setting - A fortnight or so later, near Jericho.

Scene Three – The Israeli soldiers assemble outside the city just beyond the reach of the archers on the walls of Jericho. The sounds and agitation of citizens and soldiers rushing to prepare for battle fill the air with urgency, noisy clatter, and dust. Midway between the walls and the center of town, at the home of Amos and Beth, there is a timid knock at the door. Amos opens the door.

Amos: Rahab! What are you doing here? Come in quick! Are you afraid to be in your apartment when the attack starts? Your window in the wall makes you too vulnerable.

Rahab: On the contrary. My apartment is the only safe place to be. You must go there now. Hurry before the battle begins. I must go find Leah.

Beth: What are you talking about Rahab? We are not to be seen at your apartment and certainly the wall with a window is much less safe than here away from the wall. Stay here with us.

Amos: Our walls are tall, thick, and solid. Our archers can cover any spot within 300 cubits. We are safe. The town is fortified with food and water. The Israelis cannot defeat us and they will tire and go somewhere with easier chances of victory.

Rahab: Their God fights for them. Have you not heard how He already enabled the Israelis to defeat the armies of two kings? Also, He dried up two rivers so they could cross through unimpeded. Our walls will not stop them.

Beth: If we are at risk, we are less so here than in your apartment.

Rahab: Not so. I made an agreement with them. Anyone in my apartment will be spared.

Amos: What!? You talked to them, made an agreement with our enemy? I cannot hear this. This is treason. We could all be executed.

Rahab: Soon, there will be no one left alive in town to prosecute us. Consider my words and come before it is too late. I am going to warn Leah, and then go back home. If you see Ben, ask him to come see me.

At a distance, but fully in view, the Israelite soldiers line up in long wide columns. When they start their march around the town the agitation of everyone inside the walls erupts. The whole town is clamoring with heightened awareness; everyone watching, on edge, scurrying for views and plans and information. In the middle of this bustle of activity Rahab must collect her family and get them into her house without drawing too much attention, for risk of discovery by others. The citizen's widespread frenzy provides her the opportunity to collect her family to her house without anyone questioning their motives. The town's folk don't meddle in her actions much anyway because they don't want to be associated with her.

Scene Four – Rahab's apartment, Beth and Leah are there, just to observe from the window. They pace, then stop to peer out the window, and then pace some more. The three women stand, stare, and hold on to each other. There is a breath robbing tension you can feel. Their heartbeats race, they sweat, and they pace even faster.

Beth: Rahab? Explain this agreement you mentioned!
Leah: When did you make this agreement with the Israelites, and how?
Rahab: Their advance lookouts came and stayed with me three weeks ago. I spared their lives and they swore to spare mine and any family member in this house with me when they attack. When they form their battle line, we must all be in this house.
Leah: How will they recognize and secure us in all the chaos?
Rahab: Do you see this scarlet cord in my window? Every Israelite soldier approaching this wall will see it and guard us.
Beth: Your father is confident in the strength of Jericho so he joined the busy action of preparing the town for battle. Also, he is stubborn, but I will show him the opposition and see if he agrees to come.

The sight of 40,000 soldiers marching around the city is intimidating enough. But now, the sound of the trumpets blasting away is more than Beth and Leah can take. Imagine the response of Rahab's family. They are watching from the window. They see the cord. They don't like being in her house in the first place, but this is an exceptional time. Rahab aggressively planned and prepared, but she could not have foreseen how difficult it might be to make her plan a success.
God surprises everyone with his adjustment to the plan. The Israelites are told to march around the city and then return to camp for the night. Jericho watches the soldiers march by, but they don't attack. THEY DON'T ATTACK!!
Rahab's family is bewildered and voicing rhetorical questions. Now what do we do? There are many questions brought to Rahab. Why are the soldiers stopping? What is the purpose of marching around the city? Mixed opinions spawn varying reactions. Communication with the outside is impossible. Rahab cannot explain God's plan. Still, Leah and Rahab sit, watching, waiting, and wondering.

Leah: That's it?! What are they waiting for? What is all this trumpet blowing and marching all around the town just for show? Why don't they do something already!?
Rahab: (Watching out the window with her mother and sister) Maybe they are going for weapons. Be patient and wait.
Beth leaves to find Amos.

Scene Five – Rahab's apartment, Day two. We witness the same performance by the Israelites and the same preparation by Rahab. She is certain; this is the day; yesterday was just a practice. She convinces her family and they rejoin her in her home. Beth has convinced Amos to come see. Everyone back to the window to watch, the door securely barred. Rahab must reassure her family that the plan will still work and secrecy is serious. It is a life or death imperative. Again the soldiers march around Jericho, and then go back to their camps. Again, family members stare and raise questions of doubt.

    Amos: (Somewhat gruffly) Now do you see? They know they cannot take Jericho.
    Rahab: This unexpected behavior is not their doing. This comes from their God.
    Amos: Is it not enough to turn your back on your people? Must you also abandon your god? These people will go away to easier targets. We are safe.
    Leah: But dad. All over town people are talking about how their God fights for them. They win in surprising ways and take over the lands. When did our god ever dry up a river? Remember the curses cast on the Egyptians when Moses met with their Pharaoh! If we don't join with him we will die.
    Amos: If their god is helping them, why do they wait to attack?

    Days four, five, and six come and go. No one can explain it. The Israelites march around but don't approach. Are they waiting for the arrival of something more? The guards inside Jericho laugh and in increasing numbers, most don't even race to the wall when the Israeli march begins. They conclude the march is just a show and their city wall is deemed impenetrable. Doubt and apathy seep into Rahab's family and by day five it is hard to persuade them to once more seek refuge in her home. Their faith is dimming and the daily flush of adrenaline is exhausting everyone inside the town.
    Day seven; this is the day that Jericho will fall. The usual daily life routines, commodity trading, food preparations, etc, are beginning to return inside the walls. The residents are growing impatient. "If you are not going to attack, then go away so we can return to working the fields outside the walls".
    Again the march begins, but something is different. The Israelites are marching around a second time today, and word races through town, "come to the wall and see." But still they do not attack. They march around four, five, six times and soon, the mocking starts up again. The soldiers on the wall are taunting with jeers and shouts. When the march repeats in the same day, Rahab is sure this is it and rushes off to collect her family. Imagine her hushed and fervent speech. "Yes they've marched around before and nothing happened, but today they are on their third trip around. Quick! Come and see."
    Unfortunately now, because the Israelites are repeating their marches, there are soldiers on the wall in mass numbers. But because the attack is still delayed, the soldiers have idle time and a couple of them notice Rahab. They talk together and they recall the spies who came to her a few weeks back. They saw her race about town every day and bring others to her home in the wall; her home in the wall? Does she have a window? Are they trying to escape? Three soldiers move to a lookout tower on the wall a short distance out and above her apartment and lean out to look down. Then they spot it, an open window in the wall. If that is her apartment, this is an extreme security violation with an opposing army posturing for attack. The soldiers race to the stairs and descend. They hadn't realized how many doors open to the inside of this floor. They are trying to calculate the distance from the stairs to her window, and frantically pounding on every probable door. Their shouts grow closer, "Open up in the name of the king!" The soldiers are now pretty sure which door they seek and begin ramming and pounding on it. Rahab

is not sure her door is rage tested and soldier proof. Suddenly, the pounding stops and stern shouts start up. Rahab and Leah recognize one of the voices. It's Ben.

Ben: (Talking to the soldiers pounding on Rahab's door) You there! Cease this minute! This is not necessary. You are needed on the north wall for reinforcement. Go now. I will take care of this problem.

The pounding stops, the dust settles, footsteps race away. Ben remains in the hall. Rahab and Leah stand just inside with their ear to the door. In a moment a quieter tapping sounds soft and low. Rahab opens the door unsure of what to expect or how to prepare. What courage! Ben rushes in.

Ben: Secure the door. Tell me what is going on. Nearly everyone in town has taken to the walls to watch. The Israelites are just finishing their seventh march around the city.

Rahab: Seven! Seven is a number that is Holy to the Israelites. This must be it. Quick, come to the window and watch now how deliverance comes.

Picture the attack. Joshua 4:13 tells us forty thousand armed men crossed the Jordan to the plains of Jericho for war. If they all lined up around the perimeter of the city of Jericho, and if the marching distance was one and a half to two miles, there would be 4 to 5 soldiers side by side the entire distance around the town. On lap number seven, when the soldiers stopped marching and turned to face the city, the sight from the walls would be enormously overwhelming. Rahab's whole family is standing at her window watching the soldiers prepare for attack.

Rahab: This is it! This is it!!

Leah: Is the cord visible? I'm going to hold it up high for them to see.

Then we hear the shout from all directions and see the rush of approaching soldiers. Rahab's apartment suddenly feels like a runaway chariot traveling down a washboard road, with six inch ruts. Everything is shaking, pots fall and bang, chairs skip across the room, and everyone hits the floor. The air is filled with the sounds of cracking beams, screams of citizens, and a roar like a thousand camels stampeding a small village. Dust blasts in under the door and wafts over the roof and into the window. The shouts of the soldiers grow louder. Amos leans out the window to see; can he comprehend this unbelievable sight? Not one advancing soldier has fallen as victim of the archers. Only Rahab's apartment stands intact. The entire town and all of the walls have collapsed into rubble. Amos looks down to the thousands of soldiers below Rahab's window. Two men standing in front of them call out, "Is Rahab home?"

Conclusion

Rahab experienced a change to her career, home, nationality, leadership, deity, and purpose. Imagine her courage. She risked her life to protect the spies who came to her and she risked the same to save her family from annihilation during the attack. She is listed in the ancestry line of David and Jesus in the book of Matthew, chapter one. She is held up as an example of faith in the book of Hebrews, chapter eleven. She is forever held in high esteem and talked about by Israelites visiting around the camps and chatting by the fires. I honor her bravery, wisdom, and determination.

Ruth

Introduction – 1270 – 1300 BC

Ruth is from Moab, and the author of Ruth refers to her five times as "Ruth the Moabite." The title contains an element of derision. Israel and Moab share a history of conflict beginning when the Israelites left their wanderings in the desert and approached the region of Moab to pass through to the land promised to Abraham (Numbers 22 & 23). At that time Balak, the king of Moab, attempted to get Balaam to put a curse on Israel. The resulting friction, which often elevated to war between the two nations, rose and fell numerous times after that.

We follow the family of Naomi from Bethlehem to the land of Moab where Naomi's sons marry Moabite women. After Naomi's husband and sons die, she returns to Bethlehem. Her daughter-in-law Ruth, after declaring lifelong allegiance to Naomi, returns with her. Ruth is well aware that her nationality is not in her favor, calling herself a foreigner (Ruth 2:10), but she succeeds in improving her image to the residents of Bethlehem.

Naomi works to protect and guide Ruth and determines to have a close relative provide for her. Ruth says, "I will do whatever you say" (Ruth 3:10) and eventually marries Boaz. It is a marriage made in heaven when you consider that Boaz and Ruth are in the ancestral line of David and Jesus (Matthew 1:5).

Bible account in the book of Ruth

Ruth marries one of Naomi's sons, but he dies leaving her childless. (1:4-5)

Naomi learns the famine in her homeland is over and she prepares to return. (1:6-7)

Naomi tells both of her daughters-in-law to return to their parent's home because she is returning home to Bethlehem and is not likely to have any more sons they can marry. (1:8-15)

Ruth refuses to leave Naomi and makes a vow she is remembered, studied, and honored for even today, three thousand years later. She says, "Don't urge me to leave you or turn back from you. Where you go I will go, and where you stay I will stay. Your people will be my people and your God my God. Where you die I will die and there I will be buried. May the Lord deal with me, be it ever so severely, if even death separates you and me." (1:14-18)

Ruth and Naomi return to Bethlehem. (1:19-22)

Ruth suggests she should work in the nearby fields and pick up after the harvesters pass through. According to Deuteronomy 24:19 – 20, the harvesters were to pass over a field only once and anything they missed or left behind was available to the "foreigners, fatherless, or widows." Ruth certainly qualified and applied the rule. (2:2-3)

Boaz meets and greets Ruth, gives her permission and instructions to stay on working with the other women, and expresses gratitude for her support for and allegiance to Naomi. (2:4-18)

Dialogue between Ruth and Naomi emphasizes the blessings of provisions and safety the Lord has provided to them through Boaz. (2:19-23)

Naomi prepares Ruth to approach Boaz for a possible permanent arrangement. (3:1-4)

Ruth employs the plan; cleaned up and well dressed she quietly steps to Boaz while he sleeps, uncovers his feet and lies down. When he realizes the meaning of her actions he offers to provide for her either through another family member or himself. (3:5-25)

Dialogue between Naomi and Ruth reinforces the optimism of both of them; the matter will be settled swiftly and Ruth will be provided for. (3:16-18)

Ruth marries Boaz and gives birth to a son, permanently placing her in the family line of David and Jesus. (4:9-13)

Study Questions

1. Ruth, a Moabite, marries a foreigner. Is it possible that her family feels offense and that is one reason she doesn't want to return home after her husband dies?

2. Read chapter one verses 16 & 17. What do you believe prompts such a significant declaration of devotion from Ruth?

3. Why do you expect the author of Ruth referred to her several times as "the Moabite"? See 1:22, 2:2, 2:6,21, 4:5,10

4. A moment of humor for us. Read Ruth 3:3 – 9 & 13 – 14. Notice that Ruth washes up, puts on perfume, goes to lay at Boaz's feet, and leaves in the dark of early morning so no one knows she was there. She is gone, but quite possibly has left a small portion of the aroma of perfume on Boaz. When the other farmers wake up and get a whiff, "Say, uh, Boaz, what is that new smell?"

5. Discuss the symbolism present when Ruth says to Boaz, "Spread the corner of your garment over me," (Ru 3:9).

6. What implications can we guess are true from Ruth 4:13?

7. Read Ruth 2:10 & 13 and highlight the qualities of her personality.

8. Boaz points out that Ruth had not run after younger men (Ru 3:10). Do you think Ruth knew she had that option?

9. From 2:8 and 3:10 do we get a feeling for age difference between Boaz and Ruth?

10. In Ru 3:10 – 13 we get the impression that Boaz would be very pleased to marry Ruth. However, in Ru 4:4 the closer guardian-redeemer suddenly seems to be the one to do so. With that in view, consider Ru 4:5 – 6. Do you think Boaz employs a hopeful strategy by mentioning the addition of Ruth?

Lessons

1. Ruth stood tall as a shining model for us to imitate. Her words and deeds worked together in smooth harmony. Her declaration to Naomi included the full scope of her life; she worked hard to help provide for their welfare, and she addressed everyone from a humble disposition.
2. Ruth proclaimed 100% commitment to Naomi. (Ruth 1:16-17) Her words are powerful, and today they are quoted as a high standard of loyalty to family and God. Ruth offered every area of her life to Naomi. That is the same devotion God asks of us. Jesus said, "Love the Lord your God with all your heart, all your soul, and, all of your mind" (Mt 22:37 & Mk 12:30). Her dedication, and ours, involves not just every area of life, but also every minute. Ruth's devotion was to her mother-in-law, ours is to God. Her deeds matched her words, and when our deeds match our words it shows up as consistent church attendance, regular Bible reading, and daily prayer. Then, our connection with other people is marked by love, mercy, forgiveness, and generosity, every day. Ruth's life and ours hold a strong parallel. Ruth left everything behind to be with Naomi and we leave everything behind to be with God.
3. Ruth worked hard to help provide for herself and Naomi. Ruth 2:2, 7-17 tell us she asked to go work in the fields. She worked continuously all morning, and then worked on into the evening, on her own initiative. The Bible recommends we give ourselves to work that helps provide for ourselves and others (Ephesians 4:28b & 2 Thessalonians 3:6 – 10).
4. Ruth approached people and situations with humility. We can see this in at least three instances. First, she asked Naomi, "May I work in the fields?" (2:6). Second, she asked Boaz, "Why have I have found favor with you?"(2:10). Third, she slept at Boaz's feet, (3:7).

Imagine That

1. We first meet Ruth during very happy times; she had a husband, a mother-in-law, and brother and sister in law. Suddenly, she must survive a deep shock and live with grief. In a short amount of time she is left with only one companion, her mother-in-law, Naomi. The anticipated response would be to return home to her family, mourn her loss, and then move on hoping for another husband someday.
2. Ruth must weigh the pros and cons of returning to her previous way of life compared to following Naomi to her relatives in Bethlehem. This is where Ruth shows herself wise, cautious, and decisive. We don't know what her previous life was like, but she did, and she determined to give all of herself to a future with Naomi. There was no timid hesitation and no uncertain delay in choosing.
3. Ruth is open to the leading of the Lord and certainly God is moving her in the direction He is providing. There were other fields to choose from, but she selects the one owned by a relative who can redeem both her and Naomi. Neither Ruth nor Naomi realizes God's hand is active in this until their conversation at the end of the day. Ruth did not know the field she worked in was owned by a relative and Naomi did not know where Ruth worked (2:19 -20). God is in control, always.

4. Ruth is courageous. Unaccompanied, she enters the barley fields and requests permission to pick up grain after the harvesters move on. There is a potential danger for Ruth. Both Boaz and Naomi address this possibility; Boaz tells her he has instructed the men not to touch her (2:9) and Naomi says it is good for Ruth to work in Boaz's fields because in someone else's field she might be harmed (2:22). We get to appreciate Ruth's courage when, during her conversation with Boaz, she says, "you have put me at ease by speaking kindly to your servant" (2:13).

5. Ruth is attractive for several reasons including her humility and hard work (2:7), and her devotion to family (2:11). Additionally she must be appealing as a woman with a certain amount of visible beauty. This is why, when she in total humility, approaches Boaz for marriage, he says, "This kindness is greater than that which you showed before. You have not run after younger men" (3:10). Boaz recognizes the fact that she is accepting him, offering herself to him, an older man, which she did not necessarily have to do. He sees in her the ability to attract a younger man, and so Ruth's approach to Boaz is very complimentary.

6. Apprehension of the unknown again haunts Ruth (3:12 – 18). She knows Boaz; she has witnessed his appearance, demeanor, status, and generosity. She accepts the idea she may be the wife of, and bear children for, Boaz. Then suddenly she learns there is another relative who may take his place (3:12-13). Who is this unknown relative who may come to literally own her? Is he kind, considerate, and charitable? Or, what if he is gruff, selfish, and indifferent to her? She gets the heebiejeebies and Ruth must calm her fears (3:18). At least she knows this unknown redeemer can only own her if he has some amount of wealth and that means he is likely self disciplined and a hard worker.

7. As we leave Ruth and Naomi, we are pleased to know they have great joy in their hearts. Boaz, a caring and wise man, marries Ruth; she will be provided for, protected, and loved. Ruth gives birth to a son which delights Naomi, carries on the family line, and rejoices the women who know Naomi.

A Short Narrative

The Journal and Journey of Ruth

When I was ten and twelve, my life was drastically restricted. Our full time focus was on family survival, preparing food, caring for the home, and making clothes. Once or twice each week I heard about our god, Chemosh. When a girl is young, she is usually inexperienced in much other than the daily commotion in her own home. With little outside influence, it rarely entered my thoughts to doubt the gods of our fathers.

Five issues filled almost all of our activities and conversations. The quantity and quality of our flocks, the weather's affect on our crops, how to appease our god, making new clothes, and "What's for dinner?" There was very little time for socializing, and when there was any, close supervision limited much exploration for new contacts. In our village, I knew a few female friends and shared brief visits and chats in the fields or at the water well. Acquaintance with, or thoughts about, boys, never!

When I hit fourteen, something changed. A boy came into my view and I noticed him. I actually allowed my gaze to linger and my heart to wonder. From that day on, my awareness increased, but I could not allow an increase to my lingering gaze. Instead, I found myself frequently scanning the area and could catch a brief passing glance. Something inside me woke up and it was, oh my, very warm. These passing glances kept on for days and then weeks, but I could not speak of it to anyone. Just a fast peek or mom would know, dad would know, god would know, and worst of all, the boy would know.

His name is Kilion and his family recently moved to our village. They are from Israel, and all my life I have been told to keep a distance from them. However, I met his mother at the well and she is surprisingly pleasant and kind. Her name is Naomi. When I learned they are from Israel, I began to watch for how my neighbors interact with them. Apparently, most people observe, in varying degrees, the "keep a distance" requirement. Most of my support for that restriction buckled after just a short chat with Naomi at the well, and oh, Kilion her son is so handsome. In this respect I am not alone. Orpah, a young girl in our village, has shown some strong attachment to Kilion's brother.

A year into the presence of Naomi and her husband, and Kilion, I find they are much more welcome in our town. Folks have accepted their conversations and they share territory for grazing. Kilion and I are taken with each other, but it is still so covert that it amounts to little more than greetings and smiles. My mother and sister suspect my affections, but say nothing. I see it in their eyes when he passes in the street and they watch me. At my age, I was yet to realize the intensity of cultural differences. But my mother and sister knew, and that is why they studied my reactions to him. The Israelites and Moabites do not see gods, sacrifices, and ceremonies the same and sometimes there are sour disputes. Our histories are packed with conflicts resulting from our views.

At sixteen, full of love and rebellion, and with a hopeful vision for the future, I married Kilion. For weeks my father would not speak to me, my sister hangs her head and sighs, and my mother prays for me. Now I must face two gods and two families and a husband. It is not as dreamy as I had hoped. Imagine my apprehension, where did I get the courage? Protests are always sharpest in the beginning. Kilion's family warms to me much earlier than my family warms to the marriage. I spend a lot of time with Kilion's family and am surprised to find how soon I let my guard down. They treat me to kindness and support I rarely ever see or hear anywhere else.

In my home, when god entered our thoughts or discussion, a thick gloom came with it. It seemed a common fear always came over us in those moments. In Naomi's home, it is very much the opposite. They joyfully look forward to the presence of their God. In prayer, they invite him to their meals, conversations, worship ceremonies, work spaces, and their bedrooms. I am gradually migrating toward their God and a heavy load seems to be falling off my back.

A few years have gone by and there are many changes. An illness swept through many villages and took the lives of so many close friends and relatives. Orpah and many other women lost their husbands. The night air is bitter with the sobs of sadness. The energy in our town collapsed. We all move about with swollen eyes, tender touches, and hugs. Now my husband is sick also, and I am terrified. We've been married such a short time and haven't yet started the family we dream of. I can think of nothing but being right there by his side.

When I woke up this morning, Naomi was standing there; she was very quiet and hung her head. I knew what it meant. Naomi, Orpah, and I can barely breathe. No one can speak. There is nothing to say. Three women, sharing love and laughing last year, then widowed this year. None of us know where to turn.

A few weeks pass and we tend to the mere basics of survival. Today I see something new in Naomi. No longer hanging her head low, she is staring off into the future. She says a travelling merchant came by the village last night and he reports that the famine in Israel has recovered. As a sole foreigner here now, I am certain she is considering a return to her homeland. She is the only positive female role model I've ever had. She is always considerate and kind. Deep in grief must I now face losing her too? I consider my options. If I go with Naomi to Bethlehem I will feel so disconnected. I will not know the people or their ways. If I remain in Moab, my family and village will treat me with mild contempt. My best choice is an alliance with Naomi, a new life and a fresh beginning. I know I can trust Naomi and her God.

Conclusion

"Your people are my people, your God is my God, Where you go I will go" (1:16-17). Such a degree of love and loyalty, attributed to Ruth, is quoted somewhere in the Christian world every day. It represents the highest standard of loyalty and faithfulness we can claim, pursue, and live up to.

Intuitive wisdom guided Ruth's choice to follow Naomi's God. Naomi claimed God turned his hand against her and yet she remained loyal to him. Ruth understood the power of that dichotomy. The exact same issue should serve to reinforce our faith in God. When we listen to the leader's prayers in church, or Sunday school, or home Bible studies, and we hear about really painful or difficult situations, take special notice of the overwhelming crazy love the people involved still maintain for God. Rejoice and marvel that God can step out of the way and allow hurt and still be so intensely loved.

In Ruth we find a completely humble surrender. In her actions and words, Ruth gave herself first to Naomi, and then to Boaz; she took the disposition of, "all I am and have is yours to direct and use." I will trust and accept every plan you have for me. You have my full support. I will not allow my preferences to interfere with yours. That is exactly how God wants us to come to Him.

Samson's mother

Introduction – 1100 – 1200 BC

Even Samson had a mother. (Ancient Rabbinic tradition identifies the mother of Samson, and the wife of Manoah as the "Hazelelponi" mentioned in 1 Chronicles 4:3, Wikipedia). Therefore, with a shortened version, for simplicity, and with respect, I refer to her in this chapter as Hazel, a truly beautiful name.

We first meet Hazel in chapter 13 of the book of Judges. We are not told her name there, but we do get to walk with her through several amazing moments. She is met by an angel who prophesies a childbearing future for her. During the angel's subsequent visit, Hazel witnesses two miracles with her husband by her side. She indeed bears a son and will raise him with very strict guidelines which will be watched every minute by God himself. Her commitment contributes to her son changing the history of Israel in a way that will be recounted innumerable times in Sunday school classes all over the world.

Bible account in the book of Judges, chapters 13 and 14

Hazel was childless, unable to give birth. (13:2)

The angel of the Lord appeared to her and said, "You are barren, but you will become pregnant and give birth to a son." (13:3)

The angel commanded her, "Now see to it that you do not take any fermented drink. Your son will be a Nazarite, so no razor may ever touch his head." (13:4-5)

She told her husband all about it and he prayed for the angel to return and teach them how to raise their son. (13:6-8)

The angel returned and described the requirements. (13:9-14)

Samson's parents prepare an offering to the angel and the angel ascended to heaven in the flame from the altar. (13:15-21)

She reasons with her husband that though they have seen God, he will not kill them because he accepted their offering. (13:22-23)

She raises Samson as required and he grows strong in the Lord. (13:24-25)

Samson's parents participate in securing a Philistine woman to be his wife, but they protest the plan from the beginning. (14:1-5)

Study Questions

1. What did the mothers of Isaac, Samson, Samuel, John the Baptist, and Jesus have in common?

2. Specifically, what did Elizabeth and Hazel have in common about how they would raise their sons?

3. In 13:6 Hazel reports, "A man of God came to me. He looked like an angel of God." Do you think she was calm or flustered? How would you respond?

4. Hazel's husband Manoah prayed for the angel to return and teach them. In 13:10 Hazel reports, "The man who appeared to me the other day!" Why do you believe the angel took a few days to return?

5. Who trusted Hazel more, Manoah or the angel? Consider Manoah's request for the angel to return and the angel's response to Manoah. ~~Ge~~ Judges 13:8 - 14

6. During the encounter with the angel what frightens Manoah? Why is Hazel calm about the meeting? Judges 13:17 - 23

7. Who knows more about the ways of the Lord, Hazel or her husband?

8. Hazel and Manoah witness an angel of the Lord ascend toward heaven in the flames of a fire. How well would that go over with you?

9. Samson asked his parents to get him a wife from the Philistines. Why did that bother his parents?

10. How assertive are you when your children ask for anything that is clearly in opposition to the preference of the Lord?

Lessons

1. Faith and trust. Jesus tells us to accept the gifts and presence of heaven with the simple faith of a child (Mark 10:15). Hazel does just that. When the angel met with her and told her the good news that she would have a child, she didn't conduct an inquiry. She didn't ask him where he came from or on whose authority. She just accepted the message and went home. She did report that the messenger looked like an angel and of course that may have contributed to her faith. However, when Gideon and Zechariah were met by angels with good news messages, they both expressed skepticism and challenged the angels. We are to greet news from heaven, in whatever form it appears, with the faith of a child.
2. Habit. Hazel was in contact with God continuously enough to recognize the majesty of the situation. The angel said, "Your son will be a Nazarite." She was familiar enough with that title that she didn't ask for an explanation. That means she was keeping well aware of the laws of God and ready to take action when called upon. She was practicing the presence of God in her life at a time when such dedication was forbidden. Remember, Israel was under the rule of the Philistines and they forbid the worship of any deity but theirs. Hazel was in the habit of inviting, looking for, and interacting with the presence of God. It should be our way of life too. In each important instance, we should be asking, "Lord, what would you do or say right now?" We should start now, or diligently continue to practice the presence of God. Pray regularly, read the Bible daily, and look for evidence that God is making improvements around us all the time. Then, when God shows up in your day, you will be ready to accept and participate.

Imagine That

One of the most familiar Bible stories is about Samson and his conflicts with the Philistines. We remember the images of him burning down their crops, his trust of Delilah, the loss of his strength, his capture, and at last, the day he toppled their coliseum. His remarkable escapades attract our attention and we write books and make movies about him. Next to Samson, his parents get lost in his shadow pretty quickly. But, because I want to honor his mother, I take you now to examine her story and the psychological challenges she endured. Consider the following passages in Judges.

Hazel was barren. (Judges 13:2) That truth weighed her down with a mixture of shame and disappointment. When Elizabeth, the mother of John the Baptist, became pregnant with John, she said the Lord had taken away her disgrace among the people (Lu 1:25). Hazel felt that same disgrace. When Hannah, the mother of the prophet Samuel, could not conceive, she stood weeping and praying in the temple (1 Samuel 1:10). Hazel could relate; she too was hurt, and every month her menstrual cycle again brought her renewed disappointment.

Hazel is startled. (13:3-5) An angel appears to her and brings her great news with two shocking features.

First, she will at last conceive and have a son. She trusts the messenger, feeling "he looked like an angel of God". This fills her with great joy. Second, the messenger says her son is to be raised as a Nazarite. This term may be familiar to Hazel from the writings of Moses. Even if so, the angel still tells her two requirements she must observe, first, what she must not consume, and second, you may never cut the boys hair. Hazel only wanted to be a mom, and now she is going to be a 'someone special' mom God will watch every day. Now that might be just a little stressful.

Hazel is pacing on the inside. Her husband prayed for the messenger to return and teach them how to raise their future son. (13:8-11) But, Hazel doesn't know for sure when, or if, the angel will return. Therefore, until he does, Hazel will be looking over her shoulder every minute. Every bump in the night, every brush of the wind, every shifting shadow, or the sound of any new voice, will send her heart racing and her voice anxiously inquiring, "Who goes there?" We know a few days pass because of verse 13:10 where, when the angel returns, Hazel reports, "The man who appeared to me the 'other day'." So, while she waits, she wonders and replays his words in her memory.

Hazel is brave. After the angel delivers the message a second time, Hazel and her husband watch the angel ascend heavenward in the flames of their fire (13:20). Hazel does not lose her self-control or her clear thinking. She remains composed and undaunted. Imagine her courage.

Hazel is wise. Her husband exclaims, "We are doomed to die! We have seen God." At a time when Israel is under the rules of the Philistines, Hazel remains fluent in the teachings of Moses and the ways of God. She tells her husband, "If the Lord had meant to kill us, he would not have accepted our offering. (13:22-23)

All these events weigh on Hazel's thoughts and adjust her peace of mind. She is not a timid woman. She enthusiastically prepares for the obligations and rewards of her new important role. But, never far from her daily plans are the extra words spoken by the angel regarding her son 13:5b, "He will take the lead in delivering Israel from the hands of the Philistines." That is a really big responsibility for Samson, and Hazel must help prepare him for that ability.

Yet one more shock awaits Hazel. When Samson is a man, he will choose a wife from the Philistines, an absolute violation of God's laws, in the eyes of Hazel. Dutifully she attempts to dissuade him, but without success. We hope she did not blame herself for Samson's choices or question her efforts to guide him. The best rearing in the world cannot guarantee a child will always choose the best paths, and God was using this choice to confront the Philistines.

I honor Hazel because the Bible honors her son. So, she certainly did a lot of the right things to get him there.

A Short Narrative

My name is Manoah and I have a confession; Hazel, my wife, is more devout than I am. You will eventually know her as Samson's mother. She is my strength and inspiration. Please allow me to share our story.

Hazel endured two tremendous struggles for the past twenty years and remained loyal to God, and optimistic. First, she is unable to conceive, and that tears at her heart every day. Second, at this time, Israel is subject to Philistine rule and openly worshiping our Lord is strictly forbidden. With faith and defiance, Hazel maintains a strong commitment to the ways of our Lord. She follows most of the requirements even though she knows the risks.

The Lord has been pretty quiet in our land for many years. We Israelites have tried to take the land promised to Abraham, but we have not been very vigorous. Our clan from the tribe of my ancestor Dan has failed to conquer the land allotted to us. As a result, we are under the rule of the Philistines who occupy much of the land around us. This situation is awkward and dangerous which brings us very little peace. The Philistines worship Dagon and, in their territory, they rarely tolerate the worship of other deities. A devout Jew who flagrantly puts the God of Abraham in primary view risks the wrath of the Philistines. Hazel is a devout Jew.

Hazel anxiously wants to raise her own children; for many women, motherhood is one of life's greatest rewards. When a woman, for some reason does not conceive, our culture tends to place partial blame on the relationship between her and our God. Everyday this is a double sting for Hazel. She has a close-up view of other mothers with children laughing together in town and she can't think of any reason God would be angry with her and keep her barren. She had heard the history of Leah and Sarah and their account of God helping them become pregnant. So, why doesn't God help Hazel?

Even so, she remains faithful to the desires of God. She often poses questions to the Levi's regarding foods, clothing, prosperity, and relationships. She is very familiar with and respectful of all the wisdom in the writings of Moses. She is particularly stringent concerning the Sabbath, and on that day she does not work at all. Her dedication is unwavering and, as I said, she is my inspiration.

Therefore, when the angel appeared to Hazel and said, "You will have a son", she accepted his words with complete confidence and delight. His words exceeded her hopes and she literally ran home to tell me. Then some communication breakdown entered the situation. First, I wanted to hear the prophecy myself because, according to Hazel, we were about to begin a strict parenting arrangement, which would place challenging guidelines on every day with a new son. Second, for some reason, Hazel and the angel left out the original prophecy mention about our son's destiny to lead the rescue of Israel from the Philistines. Later, I wondered if Hazel was particularly hesitant to face that future, and delay those requirements.

Now here is one of the moments where I think Hazel was exceptionally brave. I however, wilted. I prayed for the angel to return and teach us, and he did. The angel came and described the decrees for a mother's diet during pregnancy and for raising our son as a Nazarite. In our excitement, we arranged an offering to the Lord. This is where my heart skipped a few beats, but Hazel kept as peaceful as a springtime picnic under a Weeping Willow. The angel stepped into the flames of the offering and rose into the sky. I nearly fainted, launched into broken gasps, and uttered something about our certain demise. You should have seen Hazel's eyes; she is so brave. "Fear not, the prophecy is proof of our protection," she says, and takes my hand. She stands watching an angel disappear into heaven and calmly soothes my fears. Imagine her courage.

So, we dove in with every pound of energy we could produce and though raising Samson was sometimes a prayer raising, nerve startling, and faith testing process, it would pale in comparison to the day Samson announced he wanted a Philistine woman for a wife. Moses and Joshua forbade marrying foreigners, and my devout wife has a son, yea, so do I, who wants to do the very thing forbidden to all Israelis. At this point Hazel must have heard a whisper from the Lord because she backed off, and Samson continued his pursuit of the Philistine. It is true a mother never stops praying for her children no matter how old they are. Every month some issue involving our son would have Hazel up pacing in the night; the Lord heard from her in words that weren't always gentle. Both her love and her faith are as vast as the ocean, but her hope still took shocking bruises.

    Hazel was additionally blessed with more sons and she cherished every single one. In my memory she wore the ribbon of 'World's best mom,' successfully achieving the conditions of raising a Nazarite and then relaxing some of the restrictions for our other children. She walked with God; just try to imagine her courage.

Conclusion

    Samson's mother portrays several admirable qualities that we could probably explore and discuss for hours. The two that stand out very large to me are piety and patience. Her piety emerges as so natural when she talks with the angel two times and remains so calm, as if she does this all the time. She knows God's ways so well that the plan for her to raise a Nazarite does not alarm her. Watching an angel fly away in the flames is just another day in the field to her. She tells her husband, "Don't be afraid, we are safe." God nurtured Hazel very well.

    Even with great godliness, Hazel is probably one of the top five most patient women in the Bible. Twice in her life she had to wait a long time for an answer to her hopes.

    First, she was barren for so long that the author of Judges wrote that she was, "… a wife who was childless, unable to give birth," as though that was her accepted condition for life. Perhaps she had already accepted that as her permanent situation. But, if she was still hopeful for an opportunity to rear her own children, every month her menstrual cycle signaled the repeat disappointment. Then, every month she searches deep inside herself for some remnant of encouragement to hope and try again. When the angel comes to her with news she will soon conceive, she is very enthusiastic.

    The second situation that tested Hazel's patience and demonstrated her courage is found in the prophecy of the angel. In Judges 13:5b about her son, the angel says to Hazel, "He will take the lead in delivering Israel from the hands of the Philistines." The angel tells her that before her son is even born, and the event won't occur for at least 20 years. Every year of her son's life up to that time she had to wonder what that prophecy would take the form of. She had to treat him special even when her other children came on the scene. The diet and hair of Samson would certainly cause her other children to ask questions and she would again face the wonder of what would happen in his life. She would have to be very durable with raising her children side by side, but differently. She would wait patiently the long years of his maturing for the day when major changes were certain. Her son would rise up against a powerful, violent nation. She would be scared of the possibilities, but resilient, knowing God was in control. Imagine her courage.

    Patience is a precious virtue, brings peace, calms the spirit, and is desired by everyone. I saw a sign in a fast food restaurant that said, "After the customer places their order, they begin expecting their food within 45 seconds." In one such restaurant, I saw a customer throwing French-fries at the employee behind the counter because he was impatient. Months later I told another fast food employee about that incident. She said, "For me it was a cheeseburger." I wish Hazel was here to teach us patience now.

Sarah

Introduction – 2100 BC

In Egypt there are reports of a foreigner in town; a wealthy woman, beautiful, and single. When we meet Sarah, her name is still Sarai. The rumors say she travelled several hundred miles from the east. She just recently arrived and already several prominent leaders and merchants notice her. Her caravan includes her "brother" Abram, several servants, and hundreds of livestock. Her name is Sarai; Sarai is without children or husband, and she is well to do. Surely, they believe, she must be in need of a husband and so she is escorted to the Pharaoh. He accepts her as his wife and she lives in the palace with him. Abram is favored because of Sarai and he receives gifts of more servants and livestock. Pretty soon something very serious has gone wrong. A major illness is taking over the palace. Oracles, mediums, and enchanters are consulted. God is striking the Pharaoh and everyone in the palace because Abram, the man that Sarai travels with, is in reality her husband. God has prevented the Pharaoh from touching Sarai, but now the Pharaoh is irate and she must leave. Abram is rewarded and guarded, and with his wife, and all their possessions now significantly increased, they return to the land God promised they would possess.

God changes the names Abram and Sarai to Abraham and Sarah. God chose Sarah and is testing her patience, trust, and faith. She first heard that Abram would be the father of many nations, when she was 65 years old. She needed much patience. At the age of 90, Sarah will finally become a mother; the mother of Isaac, the grandmother of Jacob, the great grandmother of the twelve tribes of Israel. Her grandson will be Jacob and God will change his name to Israel. He will have twelve boys by four wives. Whew! Sarah has much work to do and will need God every step of the way. At 90 years of age she will bear and begin to rear Isaac.

Bible account of Sarah in Genesis

Abram is married to Sarai. They move from Ur to Harran. (11:29-31)
When Sarai was 65 and Abram 75, God calls Abram to move to the land he and his descendants will inherit, and they proceed to Shechem. (12:4-6)
The story in the introduction unfolds. A severe famine forces Abram and Sarai to move to Egypt. Sarai is so beautiful Abram asks her to say he is her brother to protect him from being killed. The pharaoh discovers the truth and sends them away with more possessions. (12:10-20)
Sarai has pined for a child for more than twelve years and she loses her patience. She asks Abram to sleep with her Egyptian slave, Hagar, to try and build a family through her. Hagar becomes pregnant and disrespects Sarai and in return Sarai mistreats Hagar. Hagar runs away, but the angel of the Lord finds her in the desert and tells her to return and submit to Sarai with the promise that Hagar's descendants will become too many to count. She is to name her son Ishmael. 16:1-11)
God changes the name Sarai to Sarah. Both names mean "princess." But when God changes your name, he is claiming you as his own forever. (17:15)

God comes to visit and renews the promise that Abraham's descendant will be his own son from his own wife. Sarah laughs, after all she is 89 and has long ago given up hope of motherhood, and God chastises her for doubting Him. Abraham and Sarah move one more time and in the new land they repeat the old, "tell them you are my sister" routine. So Abimelek makes the mistake of taking her in. God comes to Abimelek in a dream and says, "You are as good as dead because of the woman you have taken…" I think that is the ultimate nightmare. (18:1, 10-15)

Sarah indeed becomes pregnant and gives birth to Isaac. She celebrates with laughter and says, "Everyone who hears about this will laugh with me." (21:1-3, 6)

Study Questions

1. Sarah and Abraham moved from Israel to Egypt because of a famine. In Egypt, why was Sarah taken into the palace of the Pharaoh to be his wife? How did God intervene? Ge 12:14 - 18

   _____

   _____

   _____

2. How old was Sarah when she gave up on having children of her own and took action outside the plan of God?

   _____

   _____

   _____

3. What plan did Sarah pursue to improve her chances of having a family? How did she almost ruin that plan? Ge 16:1 - 8

   _____

   _____

   _____

4. When Sarah's servant began to treat her bitterly, why did Sarah blame Abraham? Was her animosity misdirected? Ge 16:1 - 6

   _____

   _____

   _____

5. Speculate on the courage Sarah needed to move into the castle of King Abimelek and pretend she was single. Ge 20

   _____

   _____

   _____

6. Describe the shocking way King Abimelek found out the truth about Sarah. Ge 20:1 - 7

7. While deceiving the Pharaoh and then later, a King, what personal hazards do you think Sarah may have dreaded?

8. How old was Sarah when she finally did have her own child? Why do you think God made her wait so long? How long did Sarah live?

9. Sarah lied to a Pharaoh, a King, and to God. How is she an example for us?

10. When every male in the camp was circumcised, including Abraham and Ishmael, do you imagine Sarah felt a mix of sympathy and humor? Would this event enhance the camaraderie among the women in the camp?

Lessons

1. God is not in a hurry just because we are. His plan will unfold at the proper time. When she was 65, Sarai learned Abram would be the father of many nations. Believing this involved her, she had to wait until she was 90 for the prophecy to come true. When we walk with God, we must be patient and trusting. It is enough that He includes us in his plan, so be content with His wisdom for setting the time frame.
2. All women should believe God is willing to forgive and use them for his plans. Sarah at times disappointed or frustrated God and He still included her in His plans and blessed her life. Several times Sarah went against God. Here are some of them. Sarah got tired of waiting for God's promise that she would have a child, and told Abraham to sleep with her slave Hagar (Ge 16:2). Impregnating Hagar was Sarah's idea and then she gets angry with Abraham when Hagar despised her (Ge 16:5). Sarah doubted God. In Ge 18:12 She laughed to herself and thought, "After I am worn out and my lord is old, will I now have this pleasure?" Then in Ge 18:15 she lied to God and said she did not laugh. In Ge 21:8 – 14 Sarah chased Hagar and Ishmael away. Even so, at 90 years of age, she delivers her first child. God never gives up or quits, he just sets the calendar in His own special way.

Imagine That

1. Permanence is fleeting. Sarah has moved from Ur to Harran to Egypt to the Negev to Gerar to Beersheba. Each time she must learn how to live and prosper, avoid danger, leave behind acquaintances, and reacquire her hope to have a child.
2. Moses tells us early on in Ge 11:30 that Sarai could not conceive. Moses was reporting this through either hindsight or the Holy Spirit, but at that time in Sarai's life, she still may not have known if it was her or Abram who could not produce. That made Hagar a test to see if it was Abraham who needed prayer and God's assistance to become a father. Her anticipation of "promised" motherhood began at least as early as when she was 65 and probably much earlier. But she was assured at 65 because that is when Abram was told he would become the start of a great nation Ge 12:2.
3. We expect Sarah was very familiar with anxiety, stress, fear, and dread. Twice she faced the uncertainty of having to appear unmarried to protect the life of her husband. First, for the Pharaoh of Egypt in Ge 12, and second, in her encounter with Abimelek (Ge 20). This opened the door for her either having to refuse the advances of powerful leading men or accept their pursuits and deal with the potential events associated. Either option put her in very risky positions.
4. Then, you can imagine the anxiety she might have felt when her husband takes 318 armed men into the night to rescue Lot from the hands of a hostile king (Ge 14:14-16). She paced and prayed all night waiting anxiously, hoping for victory, but also dreading the potential of danger.
5. Sarah also knew humor and admiration. Abraham and all the men of his household were required to be circumcised (Ge 17:23). I'm sure Sarah heard how Abraham introduced the idea to Ishmael, his son, who was 13 years old at the time. She

likely did not envy any part of the idea or process. Just hear Ishmael, "Dad! You are not serious! You want to do what with a knife? No thanks!!" Sarah then probably shared a very quiet chuckle with all the other women nearby over the next few days as all the men moaned and tip toed about. No romance in camp this week.

A Short Narrative

Isaac still mourned deeply three years after his mother Sarah died. Close to the year 2026 BC, Isaac, at the age of 40, married Rebekah and she became a great source of comfort to Isaac in his time of sorrow.

Ten years into the marriage, even with Rebekah's continuously sincere dedication to comforting Isaac, they still remained childless. Rebekah bore the pain and the shame and grew to doubt she would ever conceive. Seeking reassurance and guidance, she went to visit Abraham. Relaxing in the evening, Abraham receives his visitor.

Rebekah: "I never met Sarah and it depresses Isaac to talk about her, so I know very little of her life and qualities. Would you please tell me about her, what she was like, how she raised Isaac, and what she was fond of."

Abraham was genuinely pleased to sit and reminisce regarding the love of his life, Sarah. He very much wanted to talk about her, brag about her, remember her, recall her voice and her laugh and, still deeply missing her, he expected his tears to fall.

Abraham: "Rebekah dear, have a seat here close to me and allow an old man to take you to the past and revisit cherished memories."

After a minute or two of silence, eyes closed, pausing among the memories, selecting the highlights to share, Abraham begins.

"Sarah was a feisty one, full of passion, compassion, and fire. I was blessed with her powerful love and was also stung a bit when I didn't take heed. Sarah was a beautiful woman and that is a double spirited blessing and curse. The blessing of course was mine, because every day she took my breath away. But the curse surfaced all too often. I wasn't the only man who treasured her beauty. For our mutual safety, when we moved to new locations, she would tell everyone I was her brother. Regarding other men, this put her in the precarious position of available, but not interested. Twice that didn't go so well and she was taken in to prepare to be the wife of a Pharaoh or King. She faced this challenge bravely and created stall procedures claiming lengthy preparation requirements. She knew that rejecting a king or revealing the truth could bring grave consequences. She was very courageous and held on to her faith in me, her strength, and God. The outcome in both situations was startling. In the Pharaoh's palace everyone except Sarah was afflicted with serious diseases and when they realized Sarah was the reason, they gladly released her. When she was taken in to live with the king, God appeared to him in a dream and said, "You are as good as dead because of the woman you have taken." So, the king also gladly released her. In both cases she hid her fear internally and stood firm. Imagine her courage."

Abraham blots a couple tears away and continues. "Sarah was exceptionally strong willed and could keep hope alive for a very long time. God told me I would be the father of many nations, and every month after that for twelve years, Sarah expected to discover she was at last pregnant. Every month brought new disappointment and every month she would again rekindle the fire of her hope. Sarah held on to her belief for twelve years, but then gave up."

Rebekah: "It sounds like Sarah and I have something in common. Isaac and I are ten years married now and still childless. I know about renewing my hope every month."

Abraham: "Sarah knew how to put her priorities second to those of the family. The only heir I had was one of my slaves and none from my own bloodline. In humility she suggested I father a child through her slave. I of course should have steadfastly resisted the idea. I was tempted, but this meant we were giving up on God and trying to run the plan on our own. That is something no one should ever do, and it didn't work out too well for us. When the slave became pregnant she began to heap abuse on Sarah. A few short years after the arrival of Isaac, the slave woman and her son were sent away permanently."

"You asked about Isaac's mother. She was remarkably strong and resilient. The night I took 300 men to rescue Lot, she paced and prayed all night until our return. Sarah was also persuasive and she helped convince Ishmael at the age of 13, that circumcision was a good idea. The day all of our men were circumcised, wailing and moaning, she bit her tongue to protect us from her quiet chuckle. She was loyal, beautiful, a great mother, a perfect companion, and fiercely courageous. She eventually burst with joy when at 90, after twenty five years of waiting, she became pregnant. She raised Isaac with such powerful love that even now, years after her death, he still mourns for her."

Rebekah: "Well even without meeting her, she is my role model and strength."

Conclusion

Could we wait as long as Sarah did before she rushed things along? She waited 25 years for her own child, but she started pushing, with Hagar, 13 years before that. Today, we are far less patient. How long would we wait for a promised event to come to be?

God answers prayer or fulfills his promises to us in His time, maybe slower than we hope, but always faithfully. He certainly did so with Sarah. Life is like that; the new house, the job promotion, the vacation, the doctor's prognosis, our children's phone call, or just boiling water. We can't wait. It is too painful. So, we try to push things along or impatiently pace. However, walking with God is different. He sets the pace, we learn to trust and wait, and the wait is worth it. Every response from God is worth the wait. We are blessed and strengthened every time he answers.

Vashti

Introduction – 480 BC

In the city of Susa, during the reign of King Xerxes, festivities are prepared on a grand scale. The King put his vast wealth on display for 180 days and it is a visual delight for anyone with the invitation and privilege to visit. They are treated to couches of gold and silver on pavements of marble and mother of pearl. Wine flowed without limit in goblets of gold, all different from each other. Then a banquet lasting seven days convenes; the king is pushing the limits of extravagance.

At the peak of all this pomposity King Xerxes sends seven eunuchs to request the presence of his wife, Queen Vashti. Seven men sent to ask the queen to come to a banquet because the king wants to put her on display. It is a very early written record example of, "come see the 'Trophy Wife'." He wants everyone to admire him because of her, one of his possessions. She says no, and refuses to come. Vashti must be aware of the risk she is taking by refusing the request of the king. Perhaps she is tired of being treated like just one of his trinkets. Even so, refusing the king can be very dangerous, even for the queen. Insert yourself into the feeling she had as the seven eunuchs departed and as she anticipated the reaction of the king when he received the news. Don't assume the king is soft. In just a few years he will give an order to impale his lead nobleman Haman on a pole 75 feet tall. Queen Vashti's mind, filled with revulsion, wages debate with her heart suggesting all the possible responses to her refusal. She stood with her decision and waited. Imagine her courage.

Bible account of Vashti in the book of Esther

While King Xerxes is throwing his banquet for his nobles and official leaders, Queen Vashti gives a banquet for the women. (1:9)

At his banquet, King Xerxes is making decisions formed after consuming too much wine. He wants to show off the beauty of the queen wearing her royal crown. (1:10-11)

Queen Vashti refuses to come to the king's banquet; her response angers the king. (1:12)

King Xerxes seeks recommendations from his experts in the law. "What should be done in response to Queen Vashti's rebellious behavior?" (1:13-15)

King Xerxes consults his advisors and then issues a decree that Vashti may no longer be admitted into the presence of the king and she will no longer be queen. (1:19)

Study Questions

1. King Xerxes commanded Queen Vashti to appear before him and his guests so he could show off her beauty. Consider the following contributing conditions. 1) The King had been showing off his wealth for 180 days. 2) As a grand finale, the King and all of his guests had been feasting and drinking wine for seven days. 3) All of his nobles and officials were present. 4) All of the military leaders and princes of his provinces were present. 5) King Xerxes was very far into too much wine and its influence. 6) Queen Vashti was indeed very beautiful. Now, which of these factors most contributed to the King's request for Queen Vashti to come and be put on display? Why do you think that is so?

   _____
   _____
   _____

2. Queen Vashti was "commanded" to appear and be put on display, but she refused to show. Consider the following contributing conditions. 1) She was deeply involved in a banquet she was throwing for the women in the palace. 2) The arrogance of the King overshadowed the Queen and she already felt like little more than a possession. 3) The King must be inebriated because he doesn't routinely treat her like a "trophy wife." 4) The women at her banquet looked to her for a reason to believe in the worth of a woman, and in their worth. If they witnessed her tolerating being treated as if she were a doormat, their self esteem could wither. 5) The wine at her own banquet had emboldened her to stand her ground. Now, which of these factors most contributed to Queen Vashti's refusal to participate? Why do you think that is so?

   _____
   _____
   _____

3. What was one of the dangers to the King when Queen Vashti refused his order? Est 1:17-18

   _____
   _____
   _____

4. What was one of the dangers to Queen Vashti by refusing the King's order?

   _____
   _____
   _____

5. Why is it offensive to a woman to be treated as the "trophy wife?"

6. Where do you draw the line between protecting your self esteem and "Wives, submit to your husbands." (Col 3:18)

7. What was Queen Vashti's penalty for refusing the request of the King? Est 1:19

8. Read Est 1:17-20. Would you agree or disagree that Queen Vashti could, with one refusal, so extensively influence every home in the nation? Do you believe that disrespect is contagious?

9. If you should be in contact with a woman who was degraded in an abusive relationship for many years, but is now free from that problem, how would you advise her during her recovery?

10. Some Greek records identify Vashti as the mother of the heir to the throne, her son Xerxes the second. If this was accurate, Vashti was in a position of honor when her son filled the role of King. Does this feel like fair and just treatment for Vashti?

Lessons

1. To all women everywhere, believe in yourself. Believe that to God who created you, you are as majestic and beautiful as the universe. Believe that you deserve love and respect and that you are as precious and valuable as any other human who has ever lived. Believe that you do not have to tolerate anyone harming you physically or emotionally. Do not allow yourself to be treated as less than equal, as a prize, or as a decoration. When Queen Vashti realized she was about to be paraded around as a symbol of how great the king was, she was rightfully offended. She held her ground, and her actions declared, "If you come to me, come with respect because I am a woman of wisdom, compassion, and courage. I am not a trophy to park on your mantle." Reverse the roles for one minute and you will immediately see the indignation. It was different in ancient times, but today, to a woman, a man may claim partnership, but never ownership.
2. To all women everywhere, if you don't have self respect, what do you have that's better? Queen Vashti risked everything to keep her self esteem strong. It is the foundation of what sees you through life. She risked and sacrificed her wealth, title, and authority to retain something far greater in value, her sense of self worth. Vashti, and you, can say, "I may have missed out on some benefits, and lost some opportunities, but I never sold who I am to be who I am not."

Imagine That

Imagine Queen Vashti's awkward anxiety. This is truly a major misfortune of circumstance. Considering the circumstances and Vashti's response, we may speculate about something going on here. Queen Vashti is in the spotlight of scrutiny from all the women attending her banquet. With no men in attendance trying to call them up short, the women may realize and feed a growing sense of solidarity and independence.

Oppressed women collected together, find and welcome the strength and confidence from their queen. With abundance they actively express mutual support when the king suddenly puts her in the role of submission. Right then, his request flies in the face of the triumphant liberty all the women can now taste. Queen Vashti is in very high spirits, her guests are deep in an atmosphere of jocularity, the food is choice and the wine is flowing. The bond between women is strong and few of them feel the absence of, or need for, the presence of men. The women are encouraging each other and listening to each other, something the women are not treated to very often. Suddenly, seven eunuchs arrive and deliver a request to the queen. The party pauses, all eyes on the queen, and the room is silent. Within this valiant move toward improved equality, the strength of their determination is about to be tested.

A Short Narrative

My name is Deborah. Vashti and I have been close friends since we were five. I held her hand during some tough times and stood near during her short moments of glory. I want to tell you why I am so proud of her.

Vashti was raised under the heavy thumb of strict parents, especially her father. She was kept busy with chores almost all day, six days a week. She had three older sisters who kept their parents diverted and edgy. So as Vashti grew up, not much love, attention, or patience remained for her. Their father kept four different bells hanging in the window, one for each daughter. After repeated use, each girl knew the tone of her bell. So did most of the village. When the girls went out to socialize, they had to remain within earshot of the bells. When father rang your bell, you had to the count of one hundred to be standing in front of the window. The whip waited for the late respondent. An irritated father can count pretty fast.

Their father chose their husbands, and Vashti's two oldest sisters succumbed to his trifle negotiations with farmer friends. Those men just wanted one thing, a baby making machine. Neither sister displayed smiles much anymore. They could certainly quote the family motto of duty and family, but their eyes betrayed their pain. Daughter number three saw their struggles and knew she was next. She watched their trials, watched her father, watched the town, and watched for a way out. She ran away one night and they never saw her again. That turned their father's eyes on Vashti like forty farmers surveying the prize cow at the livestock auction. She was confined to the house unless he invited her to accompany him to market. He watched her and paced, waiting for her to be old enough to trade off.

Then one day, scouts for the throne came to our village seeking a bride for the king. Vashti's father saw all that glittered come within his reach. He ordered momma to pretty her up the best she could and be quick about it. Then he dragged her to the city to enter the competition. He left her with this warning, "If you fail me now, you will be married to a pig farmer before you hit fifteen." He was one of the original motivational speakers. As it turned out, the spirits of the animal kingdom didn't want her, but the king did. In less than a year of preparation, she became Queen Vashti.

Whether it was fate or providence, through marriage she moved out of her home confinement into an even more suffocating situation. King Xerxes was so self centered that next to him, Vashti became almost invisible. The king ordered everyone around and the same treatment extended to Vashti. "Go here or there, get me entertainment, or refreshment, or get away from me." Back home she expected she would move on and away from her father. But this, there was no end in sight. This might be her way of life for whatever remained of it; she lost hope for a change that would bring peace to her life.

Fortunately, for the queen, the king busied himself with his self exaltation. He amassed great wealth, decorations, and monuments. This left him little time to be overbearing with the queen for very long. But when his attention turned to her, he could do no wrong. No matter how hard she tried she could do very little to appease him. She nearly had to sit at his feet and wait for his next selfish request. I loved her so for her patience and tolerance in all her people relations, but it was beyond my imagination how she put up with the king. I guess I should have seen it coming.

The week of the big banquet was planned and preparations began with earnest. The king scurried about barking orders, pacing, fuming, and acting more self centered than ever. By the third day of the king's grand feast the men virtually ignored all the wives and spent their time celebrating their grand achievements. So Vashti found herself with lots of freedom and put together her own banquet, for the wives. We have no idea what the men were active with; we just knew they weren't pestering us.

The women were having a great time. There was too much food, just enough wine, music, dancing, singing, and hugs. We found abandoned joy in our camaraderie. We listened to each other, splashed encouragement all around, and dreamed of strength and freedom. We all looked to the queen, our inspiration, our noble hope. Then the eunuchs arrived. The revelry paused briefly and a message was whispered to the queen. The queen stood and said clearly, "tell the king I'm not on display tonight". We all gasped. Queen Vashti, our model of optimism, head high, smiled and poured another wine. Our combined sisterhood, the fervor of celebration, and the drenching of love and friendship all contributed to a decision she would call the point of no return. She had finally had enough disrespect for one lifetime.

She also knew, at that very moment, that she represented all the women present and thousands more who would hear about it. If she stood her ground and refused to be mistreated, she would embolden the forty women watching her. They would go home and contend for fair and equal treatment. If she gave up, they would tuck tail and with head low, tolerate a lifetime of abuse. Their sanctity depended on her response, and knowing that, she risked everything to protect the livelihood of every woman. Imagine her courage!

The men clearly understood the potential impact of her choice. From the top down she bravely opened the door for women to expect and request fair treatment. The men of her day were not ready to adjust to that expectation. Queen Vashti became just Vashti, my hero and friend. She kept her head, in more ways than one, and captured the loyalty and admiration of thousands of women. I am so proud of her. What courage!

Conclusion

At times in our history, women dared to face men and declare, "Perhaps you are stronger, but you are not better or more important." Some achieved improvements, but some lost everything. The message surfaces randomly again and again. Women are valuable, should be cherished, and wise men will respect them.

Queen Vashti lost her title and access to the king, but retained a prominent status. She gave the king a son who was also named Xerxes. One day, a few years hence, he will be king and he will favor his mother.

For centuries following, around the fires, story tellers will begin, "Have you heard the story about Queen Vashti. They say she was brave and beautiful. She had the courage of any top tier soldier. She stood up to the king and survived to live a grand life of honor." There were certainly a lot of rough spots in her path, but she knew how to elegantly navigate into a legend. "Gather in close and let me spin you a tale."

Veronica

Introduction – 28 AD

The name Veronica does not appear in the Bible, I checked. Unfortunately there are more than 40 women mentioned in the Bible who remain nameless. Many of them are the subject of research, through many other records, which results in a name we can refer to. When I focus on one of their stories I certainly want to honor her by name instead of writing "the unnamed woman." Therefore, I introduce you to Veronica.

One of the most powerful lessons in the Bible comes to us vividly the moment Veronica is healed from twelve years of bleeding. The story sticks with us because the pain she endured stuns our imagination and is important enough to appear in three of the gospels. She was in agony for twelve years, spent all of her money on doctor cures, and still suffered severely. Then, if the physical torment wasn't enough of a challenge, the social stigma of life as a recluse certainly compounded her anguish. According to Leviticus 15:25-33, until a woman stopped bleeding, she was labeled as unclean, and no one could touch anything she touched. This was a challenge for every woman who for a week every month was considered an outcast. A full one fourth of her life she was shunned, but they could at least expect it was a temporary situation.

It was very different for Veronica as the days ran on into months. This made her very lonely, every day, month, and year, for twelve years.

In whatever location she was restricted to, she certainly heard about Jesus, and the healings he performed. In a crowded avenue she approaches Jesus while battling her own fluctuating internal balance of brave and timid and the discord of despair and hope. Ignoring the crowd's disgust, she joins the throng of those seeking the King, and touches his cloak. Her touch is so momentous that, amidst the jostle of a large crowd, Jesus stops his walk and asks, "Who touched me?" There are several observations available here and one I've never heard anyone point out and describe. Open your Bible to Mark 5:24-34, and sometime, compare the account in Luke 8:42-48.

Bible account of Veronica in the book of Mark.

A large crowd followed and pressed against Jesus. (5:24)
A woman was there who suffered from bleeding for twelve years. (5:25)
She spent all her money on doctors, but was getting worse. (5:26)
She heard about Jesus and came up behind him and touched his cloak. She thought, "If I just touch his robe, I will be healed." (5:27-28)
When she did touch him, immediately her bleeding stopped. (5:29)
At once Jesus knew, turned, and asked, "Who touched me?" (5:30)
His disciples said, "You see the crowds pressing against you, and you ask 'Who touched me?'" (5:31)
Jesus studied the crowd and the woman came trembling to confess. (5:32-33)
Jesus responded, "Daughter, your faith has healed you." (5:34) The response by Jesus is important for two reasons. He referred to her as "Daughter" and He emphasized the importance of her faith.

Study Questions

1. Read Mt 9:28 – 30 and then read Luke 8:42 - 48. How do you understand faith's role in Jesus blessing you?
   _____
   _____
   _____

2. How much preparation did Jesus require to heal Veronica? Lu 8:43 - 44
   _____
   _____
   _____

3. Read Mark 5:28. Why do you think Veronica limited herself to just touching his robe instead of approaching and asking for help?
   _____
   _____
   _____

4. The Bible does not contain any earlier event of someone touching Jesus' cloak and being healed. Where do you imagine Veronica got that idea?
   _____
   _____
   _____

5. Read Mark 5:28 – 33. Describe the emotional struggle Veronica feels with the extremes of both relief from suffering, and the fear of discovery.
   _____
   _____
   _____

6. This story contains a very powerful example of, "Lost in translation". A lot of words have multiple meanings and intensities. For words like love, know, believe, see, and touch, we suffer a loss in Bible translation unless we hunt and dig. In Luke 8:44 – 46, Jesus asked, "Who touched me?" The disciples respond by pointing out how the crowd is pressing against him and they don't understand his question. Jesus clarifies the question with, "Someone touched me; I know that power has gone out from me." This touch was different. Sure, lots of people are jostling, reaching, bumping, and touching Him. But this "touch" caught his

attention. Someone came in desperation, with faith, and so touched him as to release his power. So, about that word touch. Jesus used the word "hapto" and in Vines Bible dictionary, we learn the intensity is more than just a hand resting on an arm. It is reaching out and grasping, pulling in, and holding on to. Veronica so needed Jesus that she "reached out and held on" to Him. Her grasp was so intense that it stopped Him and released His power. She was the only one in the crowd who had that much intensity. That is how we must approach Him. We must realize and admit our desperation. Then we must reach, in prayer, and hold on to Him, and never let go. Where are you on that path? Have you identified your desperation and admitted it to yourself and to God? He is always right there waiting for you to do so. Revelation 3:20 says, "Behold, I stand at the door and knock. If anyone invites me in, I will come in…" It is up to us to open the door of our heart and ask Him in. Please share about the moment you did. It helps others do the same.

_____

_____

_____

_____

7. Now, how about you? How do you feel about Veronica's struggle and triumph? Do you feel her pain, the pain from suffering for twelve years? Then, do you relish the moment of release when she, ignoring the crowd, comes to Jesus and is freed from her anguish. Do you see how we follow the exact same pattern? Our struggle may also be physical, but more importantly, we need healing for a tortured soul. Do you have a similar tale of victory?

_____

_____

_____

8. The crowd bumping into and touching Jesus must have had needs just like Veronica, but they did not release His power. Perhaps they came with improper motives or absence of humility. Do we sometimes do the same thing as the crowd? Do we enter into prayer with poor motives or damaged faith and then walk away wondering why we even tried? How can we repair that failure?

_____

_____

_____

Lessons

Veronica approached Jesus the same way we should. She was motivated by her need for renewal, she had faith He was the answer she needed, and she came to him humbly. Her desperation and trust drove her to disregard the swarm of people and her humility limited her to "just touch" his robe.

We must always believe and trust that Jesus is always ready to release his power to help us, and we must release that power with our faith. Other verses that describe the strength of faith include:

Matthew 9:29 - While healing two blind men Jesus said, "According to your faith let it be done to you."

Matthew 15:28 - To the mother of a sick daughter Jesus said, "You have great faith, your request is granted."

Mark 10:52 - Jesus said to the blind man, "Go, your faith has healed you."

Luke 7:50 - To a sinful woman Jesus said, "Your faith has saved you, go in peace."

But in contrast Matthew 13:58 says, "In his home town he did not do many miracles because of their lack of faith."

Jesus wasn't the only one who healed when people had faith. In Acts 5:15 it is recorded that people who had illnesses, and faith, were placed on mats in the street where Peter walked past in the hope that his shadow might fall on them.

Imagine That

Veronica had a remarkable faith. She may have been the only one in the crowd with that much faith. Consider what Jesus said when he stopped and asked, "Who touched me?" Then he said, "I know power has gone out from me." Peter said, "Lots of people are touching you." Then Jesus said to the woman, "Your faith has healed you." Add these statements together and here is what we believe.

She only had to touch his robe to receive the healing power, and when she did, power went out from him. Her faith released the power.

There were lots of people touching him who received nothing from him, but probably many of them had health needs. If they had faith, they too would have pulled power from him.

Jesus wasn't waiting for the moment the lady touched him to turn on a healing power. It was always there waiting to be released by faith. Of all the people touching and bumping into him, apparently only one person had the combined need and the faith to release the power.

When Jesus turned and asked, "Who touched me?" he used the Greek word 'hapto' which means the highest degree of physical contact. He was asking "Who grasped and held on to me?" That is the image we are to match. Apparently the crowd was just bouncing off of Him, something that happens a lot of the time now. People come to Him, but bounce off and away. My friend, when we get a hold of the joy of the universe, don't let go.

A Short Narrative

To survive, I disguised my appearance, or my condition, a thousand times in the last twelve years. Almost every woman is temporarily unclean each month. While she is menstruating, most of the items she comes into contact with are off limits to everyone else. But they all know it is a "temporary" situation.

That was not true for me. My discharge continued on for weeks and my family and friends accommodated the disruption with patience. Then the weeks turned into months and everyone took notice. The disruption became agonizing for everyone, especially me. Those most near to me, caring family and friends alike, began to keep a distance. I was a danger to their health and piety.

Doctors were consulted. Every food or fast you could imagine was considered. Debates were held, Levites were summoned, incense was burned, and animals were sacrificed. Some people blamed the water, some were sure it was just the heat, some blamed me, and some blamed God. Prayer sessions went on for weeks. All of my money, energy, and patience ran out. I was a "problem" no one could solve. Then the whispering and glaring started up. I guessed they were waiting for me to die, as that could only be the next phase. When I didn't die, one night I'd had enough and left to live somewhere else.

In a new town, with a new appearance, I was elated that no one glared and whispered. I could conceal my affliction and work, but the pain and fatigue were relentless. The years moved along, I was getting gradually worse, but could still perform small tasks. I slept twelve hours every day and kept no social life. Hot baths brought some welcome relief, but they were hard to acquire. Eventually my secret got out, and in the night, I would move on again.

Once or twice a year I would build up enough money and bravado to approach a new doctor. A whole new round of foods, fasts, plant extracts, drink this, don't drink that, and "are you sure you have confessed all your sins?" I assured them I was a regular confessor. I confessed everything, even things I don't think I did.

My depression and desperation took all the energy out of me. I would sit and stare at the sky for hours, and cry. I pled on my knees with God until I grew thick calluses on each knee. I wept till I ran out of tears and then I slept. The doctors pulled their chins, friends steered clear, and God was silent. Eventually they all became sure it was my fault, as no one could think of another answer, and then eventually they all shunned me. My lantern of hope finally ran out of fuel and the flame went out. Only hunger motivated me, and even that was weak. I ached to die.

Suddenly, one morning in my twelfth year of suffering, I awoke to the sound of excited and urgent chatter near my tent. I listened closely. Rumors are skipping through town of a healer roaming the towns and hills within a day or two walk from here. I had to ask questions. "What is his name?" "How do you know he heals?" "What has he healed and what can he heal?" "Where was he last seen?" "How much does he charge?"

"His name is Jesus and he is a carpenter from Nazareth." My heart, spirit, and glimmer of hope all deflated. "A carpenter; what does a carpenter know about illness and medicine?" My tears returned.

"Wait, wait, and listen to me. There have been hundreds of witnesses. He has healed leprosy, blindness, and deformities. He has even chased out tormenting spirits. He merely speaks and people are cured. He succeeds every time and he does not charge a fee. Some say he is a god. We hear that he teaches in small towns along the shores of The Sea of Galilee."

So, three thoughts repeat in my mind over and over. "Hundreds of witnesses, he merely speaks and people are cured, and he succeeds every time." I am so hopeful I can hardly breathe. Could this work? I am terrified. This hope has washed over me dozens of times before and then failed at the moment of truth. Hundreds of witnesses; succeeds every time. My optimism increases. I absolutely must go find him.

Well into three days of feeble effort, but with a heart racing hope and soaring expectation, I reach Capernaum. The town is quiet and I need a day of rest. Something invades my dreams casting serenity and peace into my soul. I jolt awake to the sound of crowds jostling and shouting in the streets nearby. They are shouting a name, "Jesus, Jesus, help us." I start toward the commotion filling the streets that were nearly empty just fourteen hours ago. The shouts escalate, "Jesus! Over here!"

The mayhem is fierce with people shoving and bumping into each other. I search in the direction all eyes are centered on, but I don't see anyone in lavish robes and tassels. Instead, I see a plainly dressed, calm looking, young man who moves along at a mild pace and smiles at everyone. I fight my way through and get knocked back repeatedly. Dozens of hands are reaching out trying to touch him. They're calling him a king and I suddenly feel unworthy to approach him. But then I vividly recall every hour of pain for twelve long years and I muster every ounce of courage I can. Maybe if I only touch his robe; I am almost there, reaching, stumbling, crying, hoping, and, I have it. Abruptly, the creator of the universe stops walking and looks around. The dust flurries, the crowd pauses, and a carpenter, the King of Kings asks, "Who touched me?" In an instant the pain leaves me and I know I am well, a feeling I have not known for so long. I almost don't recognize the feeling of good well being, then I hear it again, "Someone touched me."

I am so relieved and happy that gratitude bubbles out of me with every breath. I fall at his feet and confess. I want to sing and dance and shout and hug; tears of joy pour down my cheeks and I hug his feet. He lifts me up and says, "Daughter, your faith has healed you." I am smiling so hard my face stings. "Daughter!" he called me Daughter. The pain is gone, the shame, the humility, the fear and torment. I am whole again.

Jesus and I look deep into each other's eyes and I feel certain I am seeing the very breath of life. He bids me farewell and I turn and walk a little and look back and then walk some more. Suddenly I'm running with energy I haven't known in a decade. I can go home. I can hug relatives and friends. I can shop in the open market. I can bathe and really feel clean. I can dine with loved ones. In two days I reach my town and within twenty minutes, I stand ten feet from my sister, staring in unbelief, frozen, speechless. Then we both erupt in joyous cheers and run to hug.

In one of the miracle moments, a woman approaches Jesus with a balance of brave and timid, and the discord of despair and hope (Mk 5:25-29). She had been in agony for 12 years and thought "If I just touch his cloak, I will be healed." She had a courage that drove her to ignore the torment of the crowd. Her faith and courage caused this carpenter, this king, to stop in his walk and address her. In the hands of Jesus, She was triumphant.

Conclusion

In person, Veronica only knew Jesus five seconds when she, in faith, completely surrendered to his compassion. Jesus reports, "Power has gone out from me." Her faith unleashed the same power that spoke the universe into existence, the same power that spoke to the storm, "Peace, be still," and the same power that said, "Lazarus, come out." In a crowd of dozens, possibly hundreds, of people, only she had a faith that released his power.

Cast your imagination into her journey home. I bet she ran all the way and then told her story a hundred times. She will probably convert her entire home town to follow Jesus. They will remember her agony and marvel that she survived the ordeal. They will hear all about the carpenter from Nazareth who helps blind people see and the lame walk.

You and Proverbs 31

Introduction – Yesterday and Today

This chapter is not about one distinctive lady in the Bible. Instead, it is about the distinguished women called 'noble' when the book of Proverbs was written. It is also about the countless women we meet today who exhibit the outstanding qualities described in the Bible, including those listed in Proverbs chapter 31. You already know many of these women and have witnessed their challenges, victories, and compassion. Most of you reading this are just like them, honorable and courageous.

When Proverbs 31 was written, their society set the ingredients of what a noble woman, and a noble man, brought to a marriage. Since then of course some shifts in gender roles have adjusted. Women now fill positions in areas of medicine, the military, police, politics, education, and a wide variety of other professional careers. This was not common in the early Bible years. In the last one hundred years as women reached into new frontiers and demonstrated expertise, we marveled at and imagined their courage.

Proverbs 31:10 describes a wife of the highest integrity as a great treasure. The next 20 verses list the actions which mark her excellence and describe in detail why and how she is praise worthy. They highlight her devotion to family, her business skills, the strength and wisdom she brings to her family, and her dedication to God. Those segments of life, marriage, family, business, and faith, are still relevant, so this particular chapter is valuable for study this many centuries later.

Bible description of a noble woman in Proverbs 31:10-31

A wife of noble character who can find? She is worth far more than rubies. (31:10)
A wife of "noble" character is praised for:

She supports her husband. He has confidence and is cared for. (11-12)
She takes care of herself and her home. (22)
Her husband is respected in their community. (23)
She is industrious and works diligently to provide clothing and food. (13-14)
She consistently cares for her home and family. (27)
Her day starts early to provide for her family. (15)
She prepares her family to face whatever comes. (21)
Her family praises her for her great love and care. (28)
She has strong business insight, invests wisely, and manages resources well. (16-19)
She makes products to sell and is very successful. (24)
She ardently and generously shares with those in need. (20)
She is confident, wise, and a great counselor. (25-26)
Her strongest trait is her love of her Lord. (30)

Study Questions

1. Which of the following is true? A noble woman A) Gets up early, B) Stays up Late, C) Takes naps.

2. Which of the following is true? A noble woman depends on A) Fame, B) Greed, C) Deception, or D) The Weather Channel.

3. Which of the following is true? A noble woman relies on A) Her family, B) God, C) Her friends, and D) Discount coupons.

4. Which of the following is true? The husband of a noble woman is A) Lonely, B) Bored, C) Unhappy, or D) Overfed.

5. Where will you find a noble woman during times of trouble? A) Assisting people who are in need, B) On her knees praying, C) Guarding her family, D) Getting her nails done.

6. Which one of these does not fit? Every woman is a noble woman if she A) Is honest in word and deed, B) Forgives easily when asked, C) Trusts God even when a situation looks hopeless, D) Encourages her husband, her children and her friends, E) Is willing to share with a stranger in need, or F) Eats enough chocolate.
   _____
   _____

7. What is one of your favorite traits you find in a noble woman? Her A) Calm spirit, B) Smile, C) Generosity, D) Friendship, E) Contagious enthusiasm, F) Time to listen, G) Wisdom, H) Patience, or I) Seven layer cookie recipe.
   _____
   _____

8. Of all of God's creations, without a challenge, women are his masterpiece. He was just practicing when he created man. In the eyes of God, everything about you is special. Would you agree or disagree, and why?
   _____
   _____
   _____

9. Which of the following is true? For a noble man, a noble woman is his, A) Best friend, B) Wine partner, C) Confidant, D) Equal, or E) Fashion critic.
   _____
   _____

10. This is the last question in this study guide. You have studied circumstances where women found great courage in themselves and faced colossal trials. In situations that reach into your heart, you are every bit as brave as they were. If a child were in danger, if an animal were hurt, if certain peril was growing, what could possibly stand in your way? How far do you need to travel to find a superhero? Just to the nearest mirror. Every one of us has a body that will get tired and wrinkled. So what! Inside resides the majesty of the universe, a child of God. Tell each other and everyone you meet why it is a good idea to dwell on the positives that were and those that will be. Now, here is the question. Looking back through this book, which three women are your favorites, and why?
    _____
    _____
    _____

Lessons

1. A noble woman is not impulsive. Verse 16 tells us she 'considers' a field. She weighs the pros and cons of her investment and forecasts the cost, risk, return, and potential. That same thinking applies well to most areas of life: Which career fits best? Where should I attend school? Have I loyal friends? The purchase of big items, like a home or car, should be thought out.
2. She does not place herself on a pedestal. In verse 15 we see she serves her servants. She treats those below her with respect and dignity. If that behavior is our habit, we can respect ourselves enough to expect the same kind of treatment from those who are higher than us. People will always have varying amounts of wealth and responsibility, but equality under God is identical and calls for each of us to treat each other as equals, with our very best respect and honor. When you extend that to others, they are prompted to do the same in return.
3. A noble woman makes her man more noble. In 1 Pe 3:1, 2 we learn that when a woman is pure and reverent, with her actions alone, she may induce her husband to being more like her. When she stands up for honesty, generosity, and loyalty, it is often contagious.
4. A successful woman does not waste time or resources. Verse 13 says she works with eager hands. Verse 15 says she gets up while it is still night. Verse 18 says her lamp does not go out at night. Verse 27 says she does not eat the bread of idleness. Proverbs 6:9 – 11 speaks about wasting time with idleness and the calamity that results. However, there is a time and reason to be still for rest and rejuvenation. For those purposes, idleness is a blessing, and not wasteful.

Imagine That

How strong is the heart of a woman? It is probably in the top five forces in the universe, and when we come close it can strengthen us like steel or melt us like butter. The Bible allows us to be touched by the hearts of some truly remarkable women. Consider the intense love driving these women.

When King Solomon says "cut the child in two and give a half to each woman." Note how we stop and our knees go rubber as the true mother says, "Please, my lord, give her the living baby! Don't kill him!" 1 Kings 3:24-26

Hannah stands praying and weeping to have a child with such depth that the priest thinks she is overcome with wine. Hannah vows to give the child back to God if she could only be permitted to enjoy motherhood for a brief time. 1 Samuel 1:9-14

While a young baby, at risk of death, Moses' mother places him in a basket to float away, willing to lose him to protect him. Exodus 2:1–4

In Luke 7:38, we read about a woman who dried the feet of Jesus with her hair, then kissed them and poured on perfume.

While Bible history is full of shining examples of brave women, we also find countless numbers of women who sacrifice for others in our recent history. For instance:

Nurses - Remember the stories of nurses who held the hands of men close to death during war. Every hospital today is blessed with women who are deeply dedicated to sick and frightened patients. They encourage hurting patients in cancer centers, intensive care units, and hospice situations.

Teachers - Consider teachers who explain math or English, will encourage, nurture, band-aid scrapes, share lunch, patch emotions, demonstrate arts and crafts, worry and fret, shed tears, and laugh out loud. Almost everyone you ask can remember the name, face, and voice of a favorite teacher who changed their life for the better.

Mothers - The absolute hardest job on the planet is filled by the person who is on the job every hour for decades. She is driven by love so deep that a child's voice calling out to her in the middle of the night, or the middle of a movie, is granted full access to her arms, ears, and heart.

Women can wear a very brave face while underneath strong emotions torment them. They can hold pain and tears in check until they no longer need, want, or have to. Consider female first responders, police, fire, medical, relatives, friends, or neighbors. Every day, thousands of women are the first one to arrive to a scene where someone is in danger, or injured, lost, afraid, lonely, or suicidal. When they recognize the intensity of the situation they capture their own emotions and put on whatever demeanor is called for to rescue the person in need. In those moments women are afraid of nothing, including hazards, weather, animals, or other people. They are the true heroes in our community.

A Short Narrative

I want you to meet a lady with a personality of elegance. Everyone who knows her is glad they do. She wears a thousand hats; friend, teacher, confidant, sister, mom, advocate, nurse, etc… She gives generously of her heart and her time. She can stand tall in the daytime, bold and fearless, then at night, admit and search her apprehensions. She learned from dignified women who mentored her.

Knock on her door, phone her up, or reach out a hand when you meet, and she is ready to participate with encouragement, laughter, a shoulder, or a silent listening presence. In this life, you may not get to hear the dozen prayers she is pouring out for you, but they are very real. She may not ever admit the thousand times she looks in the mirror and hopes she is up to the task at hand; then the face in the mirror tells her, "If you give your best, it is more than enough". Imagine her courage; believe in yours.

She faces adversity, checks her resources, and proceeds to vanquish obstacles. She faces success, checks and subdues her pride, and is grateful for victories. She does not seek a place of prominence; it is granted to her by others. She will notice you, but you may not notice her. She will brag about her children, your children, her neighbor, her husband, and you, but rarely about herself.

She will laugh, cry, sing, pray, and dance. God walks with her, and together, they sing and dance. You are her, or can be; you are God's creation of excellence.

Conclusion

Believe in yourself and write your own Proverb of success. Watch for, imitate, and promote the positive actions you find in life. Apply your best to yourself, your family, and your community. When you spot positive traits in others that reflect those in Proverbs or those lauded in our day, make a mental note to continue or begin practicing them, and practice them until they are a habit.

In the movie, As Good as it Gets, Helen Hunt tells Jack Nicholson, "Compliment me." He responds, "I started taking vitamins." After she stares at him a moment or two, she then asks, "How is that a compliment?" His answer may be a pattern for all of us to pursue, on both sides of every relationship. He said, "You make me want to be a better person." Every one of us should strive to be the kind of person others want to be like, or better for. Each of us should be constantly improving ourselves, at least in little ways, and then once in a while in big ways as well.

Summary

Courage can prompt action in startling ways. Women seeking to resolve their desperation will employ extreme measures and then succeed when everyone thought the cause was lost. In one of the miracle moments, a woman approaches Jesus with a balance of brave and timid, and the discord of despair and hope (Mk 5:25 – 29). She had been in agony for 12 years and thought "If I just touch his cloak, I will be healed". She had a courage that drove her to ignore the torment of the crowd. Her faith and courage caused the creator of the universe to stop in his walk and address her. She was triumphant.

For each of us, it is absolutely delightful when we encounter the moment a woman stands up in defense of what is right. She may be driven by love, or fright, or hope, and the fire inside her can ignite her words, her feet, her hands, or her smile. When needed, she is dauntless. Because of her compassion and her actions, a child, neighbor, friend, spouse, business, city, state, or nation, will improve and succeed.

With intention, books, songs, plays, movies, and ceremonies highlight the contributions of women to family, community, and history. All women possess that potential and are to be respected for countless reasons, and especially perhaps because God their creator loves them for who they are, no matter who they are.

I know not every woman in the Bible was perfectly respectable. One deceived and sold out Samson, two others caused the execution of John the Baptist, and in the book of Acts, one of them lied to Peter and the Holy Spirit. To her, Peter said, "The feet of the men who carried your husband out are at the door, and they will carry you out also." I'm not blind to the ugly in the world; it haunts us every day in the news. They are not the people I want to examine, so their follies are not in this book. Instead, we highlight and honor women of the Bible who astound us with their courage. We relax and cheer when they are victorious. They are timeless examples, and one day I want to meet them all.

List of Lessons

Abigail

1. We are to be peacemakers.
2. Resolve conflicts quickly.
3. Always be prepared to express gratitude and to help people.

Bathsheba

1. The sacrifices of David's son and God's son both removed sin.
2. Maintain your integrity.

Elizabeth

1. Be flexible to work with God.
2. Hold on to your faith for life.
3. Believe in yourself.

Esther

1. God will use you if you let Him.
2. Fasting is a vital part of our walk with God.

Eve

1. To resist temptation, keep a reasonable distance from the source.
2. Expect that with God's help, you can get through grief, even the loss of offspring.

Hannah

1. We are not to make vows, but must keep our word.
2. Do not take revenge or retaliate.

Lot's Daughters

1. When you follow God sometimes your opponents are inside your own family.
2. When things look bad, remember we can't always see God's long range plans.

Mary

1. Whenever you come to the Lord, do whatever he tells you.
2. God visits people in dreams. Pay attention to them and trust their message.

Naomi

1. Family is always more important than wealth.
2. Trust God no matter how bad conditions get.

Rahab

1. Be ready to leave your old life behind when you join up with God.
2. When circumstances seem chaotic, trust that God is always in control.

Ruth

1. Maintain loyalty to loving family and to God.
2. Devote yourself to diligence in all areas, fully committed.

Samson's Mother

1. Next time an angel brings you a message, trust it.
2. Study the Bible and keep familiar with God's ways.

Sarah

1. God is not in a hurry just because we are.
2. God is willing to forgive and work with everyone.

Vashti

1. To all women everywhere, believe in yourself.
2. Always try to guard your dignity and self esteem.

Veronica

1. Jesus' words, "According to your faith, will it be done for you."
2. Jesus is always 100% available to us. Just trust, reach out, and hold on.

You

1. A noble woman is not impulsive
2. A noble woman does not place herself on a pedestal.
3. A noble woman makes her man even more noble.
4. A successful woman does not waste time or resources.

About the Author

Scott Milner was born in Georgia and grew up there and in Florida. He held a career in the U. S. Air Force as a maintenance technician on Fighter Aircraft for twenty one years. New assignments in the Air Force led to additional residences including California, Washington, Utah, England, Korea, and Germany, and an opportunity to experience cultures in twenty seven other countries. He holds three college degrees, one each in Aircraft Technology, Management, and Medical Assisting. His joy and pride in life are his wife of more than thirty five years and their two sons. The Air Force teaches their NCO's to write, and so, wanting to honor the courageous women in the Bible he wrote this book. He also wrote over two dozen poems to his wife that make an attempt at romance and sometimes actually make sense.

Scott turned his life over to God in 1980 and has been studying the Bible since. His favorite sources are the New International Version (NIV), The Interlinear Bible, Greek, Hebrew, English, and Vines Bible Dictionary. He absolutely trusts God and believes the Bible, though he is not always a shining example of holiness. 1 Pe 1:15&16.

Made in the USA
Lexington, KY
04 December 2019